STAG

STAG

BRIAN PRESTON

Library and Archives Canada Cataloguing in Publication.

Published by
Itchy Palate Press
4226 Thornhill Cres
Victoria BC
V8N 3G5

WWW.ITCHYPALATE.COM

Brilliant editing by Shane Bryson
Awesome cover by Troy Cook
Lovely typesetting by Colleen at Ampersandbookery.com

Paperback ISBN: 978-0-9918618-9-7
Ebook ISBN: 978-1-7782156-0-5

Printed in Canada

Why do I want *to write this foolishness? Just to hide it away?
It hurts getting it out and then it hurts when it is out and
people see it. The whole show is silly. Life's silly.
I'm silly and it's silly to mind being silly.*

—Emily Carr, *Hundreds and Thousands*

PART 1

How to start?

Thinking about it for a minute, I can say this: The past is way too vast and complicated to get a handle on, or even know where to begin, and the future can't be known, so that leaves the present.

I'm sitting here at my dining table which has six chairs, only one of which gets sat in much anymore. Mine. The dad chair.

That pretty much takes care of the present. The chair is comfortable. It has a cushion.

Now what?

From outside comes a voice: "Go away! Get! Get get!"

I will proceed to investigate.

I am back. Here is what I can report. The voice belonged to my neighbour Klara, who was in her back yard trying to shoo a Columbian black-tailed deer into mine.

You know those bathroom mats they make U-shaped, so they curl around the sides of the toilet? She was waving one of those at it. Bright pink against her perfect green fertilized lawn.

It was an interspecies stand-off. I happen to know that doe—her name is Charlene, and I know when she feels like it, she can jump the three-foot chain-link fence between our properties like nothing. I've seen her do it loads of times, but just then she didn't think it necessary. She was holding her ground. Klara is petite, and in her bathrobe and slippers she didn't look too fearsome. To tell the truth she looked comical—one hand clutched her bathrobe closed, while the other waved the bathmat at Charlene, dangling it like a hanky she might drop for a chivalrous gentleman. You know that cartoon, right? Bugs Bunny in drag. Elmer Fudd, smitten, picks that ol' hanky up and inhales the perfume.

I was watching Klara and Charlene from my deck, which sits on my carport and casts a shadow over Klara's back yard in the morning. Later in the day, when the sun goes west and the shadows swivel east, the deck still imposes itself; it looms over what should be her private space. I suspect she resents me peering down at her like that, but hey, I didn't build this house, I just bought it, as is, and moved in. If she liked me it wouldn't be a problem. If she liked me, then I could go water tomato plants on my deck and wave to her and have a friendly chat—I know it's possible because my ex-wife used to do exactly that. But I don't have the same effect on Klara my ex-wife did.

The primary reason Klara doesn't like me is because I like the deer who wander our neighbourhood acting as if they have every right to be here. Klara hates them—they eat her tulips and crap on her lawn, which her husband Jim mows short as a golf green, so smooth the little piles of deer poop look like ball bearings on a plate.

The deer shit on my lawn too but I do not care, and anyway the grass is too long to see it. Once in a while I mow my front lawn but I don't cut my back patch ever anymore, and that's another beef Klara has. Deer bed down in the tall grass not twenty feet from her immaculately clean-shaven private property; she can watch their ears flicker while stalks of grass sway in the wind around their heads. The sight of them drives her nuts and leads her to do things like run out in her bathrobe to shoo at deer with a ridiculous piece of carpet shaped like a C, which is a perfect letter for Klara. Perfect word, I mean: The C word.

Not that I've spoken that word in years, and I don't know anyone who does. Once in a while I hear Australians say it on Youtube, but no one around here. I live among lawn-tending mind-your-own humans in manicured suburbia and it's all very proper and things are better left unsaid. As a rule I say very little to Klara, but at this moment I interjected myself into their standoff by yelling from the deck, "Hey Klara! She's not doing any harm. That's Charlene."

Klara lifted her eyes and looked at me for a second, then we both went back to watching Charlene, who is one of three does who pretty much call my back yard home. Charlene is the biggest—she's the mom of the two daintier little things, Darlene and Marlene, who are twins—Charlene had them last summer. Not identical twins, and possibly not even fraternal—deer moms ovulate more than one egg at a time, and each egg gets fertilized by a different sperm. About a quarter of the time the two sperms come from different dads, apparently. A doe has a two-horned uterus inside her, like separate rooms for the babies to grow in. I've studied up on deer, as you can see. I love 'em.

Anyhow Darlene and Marlene are the adolescent daughters of Charlene, and they still stick close to mom. In fact, this morning I was thinking it's unusual to see Charlene alone like that. Without taking her eyes off Klara, Charlene swivelled a petal-shaped ear toward my voice, keeping the other ear cocked toward Klara. You will never sneak up on a deer. They listen frontwards, back and sideways. Perfect 360-degree sound catchers.

"I'm shooing her back to your thicket," Klara said. "Go, you!"

At that moment Charlene said Enough of this Crap—she turned tail, hopped the fence and disappeared into the thicket. And I came back inside and sat my ass back down at the dining table, which brings me up to the present again.

This table could use a wipe.

"Thicket."

Klara said it with disdain, but I love that word, thicket. I consider myself blessed to have one. The back forty of my property is three quarters of an acre of wilderness and neglect, a mash-up of native west coast flora and invasive foreign weeds, left to their own pretty much for a century now. I've never done a proper inventory of trees, but off the top of my head I can tell you that close to the house are four Garry Oaks, the native darlings of our local biodiversity types, and a half dozen Arbutus on a rocky outcrop near the back end, and in between a whole bunch of western hemlock and Doug fir, a few alder, and a broad-leafed maple or two, all native to this part of the world. Once upon a time there was a clearing, a meadow, but Himalayan blackberries have rooted and crisscrossed and puffed up like Jiffy Pop into a massive thorny swath, impassable to humans. Cats and rats and raccoons work their way through there on low, tight thoroughfares, but me, I'd need a chainsaw. I'm thinking of getting out there with one this winter to cut them back, but I've been saying that for years.

It's my land, I can take a chainsaw to it anytime I like. We bought it eleven years ago, just after we were married and before prices went nuts. This house is nothing to write home about, just a mid-sixties split-level—what sold me was that big old wild chaotic hunk of land out back, and the best part is that on two sides it joins up to the slopes of Mount Doug Park, forested mostly with second growth Douglas fir. Perfect. Out the front door it's twenty minutes to downtown, out the back door, wilderness. Okay, strictly speaking not wilderness, but when you're in the back yard and see it bleed naturally into the forest beyond, it has that vibe that if you started walking into it you could walk forever, on and on through thick woods to the Arctic Circle. Except we're on an island, you'd have to swim a bit at some point. Island-hop across the Broughton Archipelago. Bring a wetsuit—the North Pacific is icy cold.

When we bought this property there was an old, untended apple orchard on the west side of us, protected forever within the Agricultural Land Preserve, or so we thought. Then a developer bought it, got it out of the reserve, split it down the middle with a cul-de-sac and threw up some cookie-cutter houses with faux-rustic fake stone fronts. So now if I take a stroll down the west edge of my land I'm looking into the back yards of houses constructed circa 2009. Round the back they drop the fake fieldstone, it's just classic stucco with a sliding glass door to a vinyl deck with a barbecue. If there's kids there's a trampoline.

If that's the alternative it's no wonder deer love my little oasis of wild here in Gordon Head. That's what my neighbourhood is called. Know what I call my little homestead here? Gordon's Head. Kind of like Howards End, you know that movie? If not check it out—Anthony Hopkins chews up the proverbial scenery as he morphs from sweet to sour, and Emma Thompson never glowed more luminescently upon the silver screen. I have a feeling it was a book first. A novel. Can't be sure though. Haven't read a novel in years. Anyhow, Howards End is the name of a house. Gordon's Head is the name of my house. It works because my middle name is Gordon. But you can call me Trevor.

I wonder am I doing this right?

Rolanda said there is no right or wrong, just let it out.

So call me Trev, actually. Nice to meet you. You already know a whole shitload of important stuff about me, but in case there are gaps in your understanding, let's go for some FAQs.

Why are you writing all this down, Trev?

Good question. Due to some personal issues that affected my workplace performance, it was suggested I get some counselling. In other words I acted out on the job. When you yell at people in a windowless office, they have nowhere to look. They feel trapped and cornered, which is how I felt when I started yelling in the first place.

When my boss Mona first brought up counselling I said, "No Frigging Way, Don't Want It, Don't Need It and I'm Not Paying for It," but then she pointed out it was on the company's dime. "I know you love free stuff, Trevor." It's true. I love free stuff. Someone puts crap by the side of the road labelled Free, I'm the guy that'll pull over and rummage for hidden treasure. Lug home a rickety shelving unit and get yelled at by the wife, except the wife is gone.

Mona said another bonus re: counselling was it could be scheduled during work hours, so I could leave the office. That is always attractive, leaving the office in the middle of the day. So I went to a see a counsellor, expecting to be ushered into the presence of some grey-beard sage with an air of kindly neutrality who would point the laser of his penetrating gaze toward the window of my soul and unlock its shuttered mysteries. All would be revealed and healed and then I could just get on with the rest of my day.

Instead of that guy, I got Rolanda. She's much younger than me, barely into her thirties, and while she is kindly and non-judgemental, she ain't up to cracking open my soul, I'll tell you that much. First impression: She needs to get her own shit together before she starts messing with mine, because when I was sitting in her little waiting room I could hear her through the wall talking on the phone to her boyfriend or husband or whoever, and things did not come across as going peachy on the home front. Not that I could make out the exact words, but her tone was aggravated, exasperated, and then sad, and then she hung up. It took her a long time to come out, and I felt like she might be composing herself, drying her eyes even, before she emerged to introduce herself and take me into her little therapy space, which was a room with four comfy chairs and a whole bunch of throw pillows on a nice shag carpet.

Rolanda has round soft brown eyes and a gap between her front teeth. Her hair is very curly and parted in the middle, which doesn't suit people with a gap between their teeth. Gap in the hair, gap in the mouth—one too many gaps for me. All women except those who are very small-breasted also have a gap in the topography of their chest, so that's like three gaps, especially because Rolanda is not small breasted, she's larger than average—okay, I'm not trying to sexualize or objectify her or anything like that, but when a woman has large breasts a man notices. They protrude, right? I mean, anyone would notice, man woman or child, right? Rolanda suggested that I keep this journal, and she told me write things down as they come into my mind, and don't edit myself. No erasing. So now you know about Rolanda's boob size whether you wanted to or not. I didn't obsess over them or anything, I just noticed their size. It's normal to do that. I'm normal. Writing it down doesn't feel as normal. In future I'll do my best to avoid writing down the boob size of other women I might discuss. Unless I get nostalgic for my wife. Hers were perfect. One of the best things about her. There were many best things about her. I do miss her, I will admit to that. Right now my ass is quite comfortable on this cushioned dining room chair but the rest of me is quite uncomfortable with what a fuck up I am.

Do you think counselling is going to help you, Trevor?

Well so far we've only had the one meeting, therefore the jury is still out on Rolanda. She is sweet though. Kindly. She often looked faintly puzzled, or confused. Several times she crinkled her brow as the saying goes, especially when I started talking about deer. I couldn't help it. I like talking about deer.

When she brought up keeping a journal I protested that writing things down like this would feel like I'm talking to myself, which would make me feel weird. As a solution, Rolanda suggested I pretend I'm writing a letter to a trusted old friend, or an imaginary stranger who is curious to know everything about me. My mind drew a blank on trusted old friends—I mean, I still keep in touch with a couple of guys from high school and a couple more from college, and we go out for a beer maybe once or twice a year, but I'm not exactly flush with buds old or new. I'm a loner, I guess you could say, so I chose option two, the imaginary stranger. Greetings stranger, or alter ego, or whatever. I'm doing my best to differentiate you from myself. Next question.

What do you do for a living?

Excellent icebreaker, considering you don't know me from a bar of soap. Here's the scoop: The office where I work is in a private Care Home. "Care Home" is a funny term—there's care there but it's not very homey. Metaphorically it's a corral, a pen to put old people in when they've become useless to society and in fact a drain and strain on the system. Best to round 'em up in one big building where you can keep an eye on 'em so they don't keel over and die alone and not get discovered for weeks. The Care Home is massive, big as a hospital, full of old souls, rickety and well past their Best Before date, but I say let's hear it for the chipper ones who still have faculties and optimism. I'm happy to see them as I wander the halls from time to time. The facility is officially called Eternal Springs and has many floors, and to keep it running smoothly takes many nurses and orderlies and cleaners and custodians, and some Administrators like me. "Administrator" is a bit grand in my case, I'm more of a clerk. It is my job to make sure there are proper numbers of nurses and orderlies, etc., scheduled for each floor at any given hour of the day. My day is taken up drawing elaborate schedules that go straight to hell whenever nurses and other people start phoning in sick, which they do all the time. So I am either drawing up schedules or I am on the phone trying to find nurses who can fill in for other nurses, or custodians on call, or whatever the case may be.

That's it. The job is about as exciting as it sounds. I could do it in my sleep, but I'm not allowed to sleep on the job.

Where I work is called the Staffing Office and it's in a basement room that is windowless, I presume because the architect who designed the place decided old people should have first dibs on the windows, which is fair enough, but sucks for me.

Here's the deal. I'm live and let live. Usually. I hate telling people what I do. That means I could never rise in the managerial world because sooner or later you need to start telling people what to do. So I kind of got stuck in the staffing office and now it's nearly two decades I've been doing it and it's too late to change. Obviously I don't consider myself highly successful in the employment arena. I have some regrets, yet I can't change my essential temperament. Not to sound snobby, but with a little ambition a man of my intelligence and ability might have risen much higher.

Do I have any standing in the world beyond what I earn for trying to be a good person? Not really. And how do I know I'm a good person? I do know right from wrong, I hope. I'm not blind to injustice, I see it all over the planet. But what do I do about it? Not much beyond giving Amnesty International 20 bucks a month. My guilt tax.

What about family? You mentioned a wife, albeit in the past tense.

I did have a wife but she left for greener pastures. That's almost sixteen months ago, and we're divorced, officially, as of just a few weeks. Some people see a link between the aching finality of divorce and me blowing my stack at work, but correlation is not causation, my friend. Stack-blowing was more fully justified and forgivable at the time of separation, given the shit hand I was dealt, but I played it with admirable restraint. Very Buddhistic was what I was aiming for. The divorce was highly amicable. I love(d) her, right? Right up until the end I loved her. So naturally if you love someone you want them to be happy, as happy as they can be, right? Well, now she's happier, happier than she was with me. I got the house, she took the kids. Our kids. Probably you think that's selfish of me, keeping the house. But she didn't want the house anyway because her new boyfriend has a fucking palace.

It's true. Snug along the rocky shore near Ten Mile Point he has a palace on a huge acreage with its own little private beach no one else can get to except by boat. I'm just stating facts. And it's all good. It means the kids are well looked-after. That makes the whole thing easier to swallow. Our parting was amicable, honest. And for now I'm alone. Just me and my three girls. Marlene, Darlene and Charlene.

The kids—I mean, the human kids—how old are they?

The girl is eleven, Melissa. And the boy is eight, Kyle. Awesome age. They are sweet and good children, for the most part. The kids come and stay every second weekend. It's good. Makes me empty the sink and clean the kitchen once a fortnight. "Fortnight" is such a great word—makes me feel British just saying it. Kind of faded out of common usage here in the colonies, although it seems to be making a comeback as some online timewaster Kyle wants to get addicted to. Eight is too young for it, apparently. Mom's orders.

If you don't mind my asking, your wife—

Why did she leave? Good question. Mostly we got along great. She'll tell you that too.

I sense you're withholding.

You are dead fucking right on that, my imaginary friend. Let me get used to writing things down first.

It's hard to describe yourself. Yolanda says, Just cut loose, don't hold back, and express my truest feelings here.

Better to stay positive.

Do you have any hobbies?

That's nicer. I like watching wildlife, especially deer. In fact right now that is my major pastime. I'm stuck on deer. Their life—it's so basic! They eat, sleep, and shit on a daily basis, fornicate maybe once a year, but otherwise they pretty much spend their days wandering around aimlessly. Humans aren't allowed that freedom, that luxury. We're expected to have goals and objectives, and create linear paths to them. Otherwise people start whispering, worrying about us, suggesting we need counselling.

Enough with the FAQs.

As mentioned earlier, Mona is my boss at work. Her breast size is irrelevant, or maybe I'm just saying that because they're small. She swung by my desk today and asked me how the "journaling" is going. "It's called keeping a journal," I told her. "Journaling is not a word."

"All right then. Trevor, how's the keeping of a journal going?"

I do like Mona. We've been working in the windowless bunker together for fourteen years now. We've broken bread at each other's houses. We've given birthday cards to each other and presents to each other's kids. She's actually two years younger but she frets over me like a big sister, like a surrogate mom. Lately she's been doing more of that. Lately I can be morose and sometimes bellicose at work. Not this time. This time I caught myself and shifted gears.

"I'm sorry," I said. "I'm a grammar Nazi, as you know."

"A stickler, anyway," she smiled. Like I already told you, my going to Rolanda was really Mona's idea, after I got even more morose and bellicose than normal and created some drama a few weeks back. Here's what happened, and I'll try not to self-justify too too much. One day I was feeling a bit unwell talking on the phone and went off my head at a particular young nurse's aide who has annoyed me several times before by phoning in sick at the last minute. Sick?

Ready to party, more like it. In fact I was pretty sure I could hear her friends in the background giggling and huffing on a bong, and I told her so, and she started giving me all kinds of lip so I told her to "shut your fucking mouth" and she told me I can't talk like that, and I told her "I fucking well can," and slammed down the receiver which felt great until I looked up to see an expression of raw panic in the face of my co-worker Angie. Angie is a bit of a fragile flower at the best of times but the absolute terror in her eyes rekindled my rage and made me want to live up to it, just for a second, like, you wanna see rage, Angie, I'll show you fucking rage, I'll pull a meat cleaver from my desk drawer and chase you around shouting "YOU'RE NEXT!!!" But of course I did nothing like that, I recovered my dignity and besides, the most dangerous thing in my drawer is one of those little claw-like things for removing staples. I took a deep breath and you know what I actually said to Angie? I said, "Please don't mention this to Mona." And did Angie respect my wishes? No. Angie ratted me out first chance she got.

Angie's loose lips led to a lot of institutional paper-passing, meetings and assessments centered around "the incident," as it came to be called. I had to write a formal letter of apology to that skanky young nurse's aide who I still can't stand, and a note of admonition was added to my personnel file. Plus Mona suggested I take advantage of counselling, so now I'm keeping this journal, which gets us back to where we were—I told Mona the journal keeping was going fine.

"You seem a bit distracted today," she said. "Anything on your mind?"

"Actually there is."

"Okay." She looked at me expectantly.

"Are you sure you want to hear this?"

"I'm happy to listen."

"I'm worried about Charlene."

"Charlene?"

I nodded.

"Do I know this Charlene?"

"Maybe. I think I've mentioned her before."

"This is someone new you're seeing?" Her face brightened—I could tell she thought it would be a great idea if I started dating, or socializing, or moving on from being sad-sack single pushing fifty.

"No, no. Nothing like that. Charlene is a deer."

"A deer."

"Yeah, a Columbian black-tailed deer. I'm sure I've told you how I have deer who live with me—who live out back."

"Right."

"Well I'm getting to know them quite well—"

The phone rang and I had to take it. Another habitual absentee making her excuses. I'm sick of it. Tough it out, people! Mona was listening to me and watching my face, so I was civil, more or less. "Duly noted" and all that. Thank you. Goodbye. Click.

"You didn't sound very sympathetic," Mona said.

"I'm not her mother."

"You used to sound more sympathetic. If people are really sick—"

"I have only so much sympathy," I said.

"You're saving it for Charlene."

I looked at her. She had a slight smirk on her face.

"Charlene is acting a bit weird these days. She's under the weather."

"And it worries you?"

"Yes."

"How do you know she's under the weather?"

"I've been spending a lot of time with her. And her two daughters. I sleep with them, out back. Near them. Like we're all within twenty feet or so."

"On the ground?"

"Uh huh. That's why I've been volunteering for evening shift so much lately—it's perfect cause I get off work at midnight, get home and fix myself some eggs, or fire a frozen burrito into the microwave, and then when I'm ready for bed I haul a couple of big old comfy rated-to-minus-seven unzipped sleeping bags out to the backyard and climb between them. In the long grass under the big Garry Oak closest to the house, I've slung a big tarp in the branches, so unless it's blowing a gale and pelting rain horizontally, I'm dry. The girls are off somewhere, foraging. I'm keeping a light in the window for them, you could say. When they wander home at daybreak they don't get spooked by me. They settle in near me. My girls."

Mona has sharp, hawk-like features, but just then they softened into a look of motherly sympathy, a look of pity, really. She felt sorry for me, no denying. "They let you get close to them?" she asked.

"Oh yeah! They practically curl up beside me. They'll come home from their wanderings and I'll be sound asleep, and next thing I know there's one of them settled down practically within arm's reach. Charlene used to be bravest, and a couple of times on cold mornings when there's frost on the ground, I've found her snuggled right close to me. Not touching or anything, but close."

"Sounds lovely," Mona said. Not convincingly.

"It is. That is trust, right? Like honest-to-God trust that no matter what happens I'm there to protect her. It feels good. But now she seems all distracted, and wants nothing to do with me. The other two are keeping their distance too."

"Weird," Mona said.

"Yeah," I said. "You mean me, or the deer?"

"Both, I guess."

We just looked at each other.

"How are Kyle and Melissa doing?" Mona said.

"Oh they're good. I have them this weekend coming up. First time in almost a month, 'cause last time it was my turn they went biking at Mount Washington."

"Sweet," Mona said.

"Yeah, Michael has a condo up there. They were skiing all winter. They love it." Michael is their stepdad, my ex-wife's new man. Not officially the stepdad, they're not married or anything.

"And what do they think of the deer?"

"Sylvie doesn't like them to play in the back, because she's convinced that deer are covered in ticks that carry Lyme disease." Sylvie, if I haven't mentioned it yet, and I know I haven't, because, well, why? Hmmm. I guess I was avoiding writing her name, but now I've done it, I see it can be done, so now I know I can do it. Her name is Sylvie, she is my ex-wife, she is the mother of my children. Anyhow, as I was telling Mona, "So the kids don't go out back to see the deer much. Which is just as well. Kyle wants to blast them with a sling shot."

"Typical seven year old boy."

"He's eight. But you're right. Savage little predator."

"And Melissa?"

"She takes after her mother the germophobe. Tick paranoia has taken hold. She likes deer, but only when they're stuffies, extra-plush and machine washable."

Mona said, "And you don't worry about ticks, and Lyme Disease?"

"Not really. I've never been bit yet, far as I know."

"Well just be careful."

"Like how?"

"I don't know. Wash your sleeping bag often?"

Charlene had a baby!

So that's why she's been acting so weird.

I woke up this morning bone-chilled and glad to be tucked under my tarp because the dew on the grass was thick as rain. It was light out, the sky was blue, but the sun was still low enough to be blocked by trees and houses. I could see my breath, which was a bit depressing because I thought summer was here and we were done with mornings that cold. Marlene and Darlene were asleep in their fave spot under a Garry Oak about forty feet away, where it's drier. First time I'd seen them for a couple of days, and I felt glad about that, but still no Charlene. I got up, stretched, and suddenly, along the little trail from my thicket, here she came, very slowly, looking thin, bedraggled and generally worse for wear. She stopped when she saw me, uncertain about proceeding, when out from behind her quick-as-lightning darted the cutest little bolt of energy you've ever seen in your life—gamboling on pixie toes, all curiosity and kinetic energy, even if her legs were a bit shaky and the running style unpolished. Awkwardly adorable—Holy shit that thing is cute! Fucking melted my heart! She did a little dance where she kicked her back legs up in the air like a happy pony and almost tumbled over when she touched back down to earth. As the sun began to rise over the house, the dewy grass shimmered into a million sparkly diamonds and her teeny little fawn hooves kicked water drops up, up and away.

Fawns are cute, and cute is usually associated with the feminine, so I decided this fawn has to be a girl and I decided to call her "Primula." If I perceive male genitalia sometime in the future I may have to change that, I guess to "Primo." But for now she's Primula.

This is how the name came to me: She was running excited little circles around her mother, and then did the same around Marlene and Darlene, who were comfortably slumped on their rumps in the dryer grass under the trees. Charlene was looking warily at me, like she wished I wasn't there, because she couldn't rein in her rambunctious clueless newborn ripping around the property. It upset her instinctively that the kid was coming too close to a foreign species, namely me. Sure enough little Primula suddenly takes notice of me for the first time, and makes a beeline to me under the tarp. She pulls up just short in the glittering dewy grass and looks at me with those dewy new eyes like I'm the most amazing thing she's ever seen, and then I see something like shyness, or timidity in the movement of her body, and the first words I ever say to her are, "Oh. Look at you, suddenly all prim and proper."

Thus, Primula. It's a flower, and she's a blossom.

She took a step forward, I think to better smell me, because deer, in case you don't know, use smell as their number one sense to figure out what's what in the world. Their sense of smell is about 10,000 times stronger than ours, according to people who know how to measure things like that. They have five times more smell receptors than bloodhounds. They have an organ in the roof of their mouth called a Jacobson's organ that is actually an odour-sorter—it takes in the overall smell and isolates different components of it, if you can imagine. We have nothing like it, so we can't really imagine. Where we go, "What's that smell?" deer go, "I'm picking up 19 percent honeysuckle, 34 percent evergreen trees, five meters that way a raccoon shat three days ago, a housecat ran by in the last half hour etc. etc. etc." With all that olfactory firepower, Primula was taking her first whiff of a human being, in this case a middle-aged male emerging from a sweaty sleeping bag all underarm odour and rank morning breath. She seemed to like it though; I offered her the back of my hand to sniff like you do when you meet a new dog, and she took gingerly little baby steps toward me, but then got spooked. I think it was the tarp—she's barely as tall as my knee so she had to lift her neck up to smell my hand, saw the tarp, and probably thought the sky was falling.

She darted back to her mom and tucked her head under her belly looking to latch on for a drink of milk. Charlene took a step away, as if to say, "Not now, kid," all the while keeping her eyes fixed on me. Certain things were private, not for prying human eyes. She took the path into the thicket, and Primula darted after, leaving me giddy and elated in the aftermath. I felt high, so happy, like I was a relative, an uncle or grandparent, like I wanted to brag about it to someone, although Marlene and Darlene were having none of it. They both just sat there in the grass, chewing their cuds, ruminating as it were. I called to them, "Come on girls, aren't you happy for her?"

Their ears twitched for a minute. Then they went back to ruminating, and I suddenly thought of something. "Hey—maybe you guys are about to pop too!" It was certainly possible—Charlene had never in the least looked pregnant to me. Soon there might be two more skinny-legged babies scampering round the back forty!

It's my weekend to have the kids. Just around 5 p.m. last night Sylvie showed up in the Beamer SUV Michael gave her, and dropped them off. I was super-eager to see them, for as you know I had massively exciting news I couldn't wait to share: Charlene had a baby! I've named her 'Primula'! Wait till you see her! She is so unbelievably cute and sweet and innocent and just, like, *new,* new and perfect, and while I love the name Primula and think it's perfect for her, if you guys have a better name, I might even let *you* choose what to call her!

That was the little speech I prepared in my mind as I saw them pull up, and there I was, bursting with such enthusiasm that it even took the edge off an ache I've developed in my jaw, which I haven't been able to get rid of despite taking Tylenols every four hours for the last two days. The only time it feels better is when I stretch my jaw forward so my bottom teeth stick out far as they can go, and then I bite at my upper lip with them. That's my default position. Kind of a werewolf thing. Probably looks weird so I try not to do it in front of others. Also I'm getting a rash on my body, especially my torso. It itches, front and back, insistently, constantly, but just a little, just enough to bug me. I'm a mess right now. But I put all that aside because I had exciting news for my kids and was super-keen to tell them, and I was waiting impatiently with the front door of the house open, beckoning to them to come hither and hear my news, but they sat in the curbside SUV with the semi-tinted windows rolled up and looked across the thirty feet of front lawn at me like I was the one behind glass, not them. They were having some kind of heated conversation with their mother. Probably over having to spend time with Dad.

They come home to me grudgingly these days. Kyle is eight and up until about a year ago he was this cute, cuddly little guy I called "Bud," and we were truly like buddies. Now he's become this petulant little prig who wants to do nothing apart from blow things up by compulsively tapping his index finger on the smudgy surface of his iPad. Sylvie and I have made an agreement when it comes to screen time—we're still functioning as co-parents, more or less—which is, Kyle should be limited to an hour a day of iPad. The reason I bring up the iPad right now is that eventually, after several minutes of yakking back and forth with mom in the SUV, the kids unpiled themselves and were herded houseward by their mom, who came right to the door with them—she doesn't often do that—and before I could blurt out a single excited word about Charlene and Primula, she said, "Kyle gets an extra hour of Kingdom Rush today."

"Oh, why's that?"

"Because he wouldn't agree to come otherwise."

"Keen to see the old man, eh Bud?"

The kid—my own flesh and blood—brushed past me without so much as a glance and zipped up the half flight of stairs to the main level of Gordon's Head, my (our?)

split-level suburban sanctuary. From the living room he shouted, "TWO HOURS!" Little twerp. Kingdom Rush is a "free" app-type game all his friends play, wherein a horde of swarthy little Viking-type invaders try to make it up a path that looks like the crushed gravel driveway of a fancy estate. Kyle's job is to stop them by blasting them with bombs from pot-bellied medieval bomb-launchers, or pierce them with arrows from a bunch of archers in stone towers who launch them by the hundreds depending on how fast you can compulsively tap tap tap. There's various other weaponry available too, including giant wandering oafs who smash the Vikings with clubs. The kid is eight! That's all he wants to do when he sees his dad! It's very sad, really, but today, for some reason, maybe because my jaw was killing me, it really, supremely, pissed me off.

Melissa was in no better mood. When I said to her, "Hey, I have exciting news for you, kiddo!" she fixed me with a cold stare, kicked off her boots, which are called "Soft Moccasins" or something, big saggy soft beige boots that all the girls age 8–22 are wearing lately despite the fact they soak up water like a sponge and are completely inappropriate for the kind of soggy west coast weather we get around here nine months of the year. But hey, it's form over function when it comes to women's fashion, I get that. "There's a new season of H2O on Netflix, and I get to watch as much of it as I want," she said. H2O is a TV series from Australia where three teenage girls try to cope with the travails of high school, boys, dating, sports, and family dysfunction while saddled with an unfortunate cross to bear: Whenever they get wet, they turn into mermaids. I know it sounds preposterous, but it's actually pretty good—it's one of those shows for tween girls that teaches them all about the value of true friendships, and honesty, and how to figure out who you can trust with a secret. Melissa watches it with intense undistractable focus, weighing every word for clues as to what it means to be a teenage girl, which at the age of eleven she is tremendously impatient to get to. The whole childhood thing? Been there done that. Sixteen months ago when the marriage fell to pieces and she went to live with Michael and Sylvie, she used to send me a stream of selfies from her mom's phone, trying to maintain a connection with me, showing me she was still loyal. But gradually she's joined her mother's camp. She doesn't hate me but she has no interest in earning my approval or cultivating my friendship. I'm just the guy who makes her do homework every second weekend. She disappeared up the stairs and turned right toward her bedroom, leaving me and Sylvie standing on the doorstep.

"Binge-watching H2O—was that her condition for coming?" I said.

"No, she never said a word about it to me," Sylvie said. "Her biggest complaint was that she didn't set up any playdates for the weekend, but I told her it's not too late if that's what she wants, and if she doesn't do it, it's her own fault and not to blame you."

"Not to blame me? That she'll get to spend time with me?"

"Cut her some slack. She's eleven, a tricky age, and only getting more so. We haven't made it easy on them. I take responsibility for that. She's not a lot of trouble—she's always been a very sweet kid. Kyle's the one making trouble."

"He's an addict. I'd love to just smash every screen in the house," I said. For some reason I made a head-butting motion like the smashing should be done with my skull.

"Take it easy, man," said Sylvie. "Are you all right?"

Behind me, up the half flight of stairs, I heard Melissa say, "Ewww! This is disgustingly *gross*, Dad!"

My precious daughter had gone to the kitchen, which admittedly was a bit cluttered; I'd meant to clean it before the kids came over, but what the hell, Charlene had a baby, for God's sake! She came to the top of the stair and said to her mother, "I can't even see the countertops, there's so much crap everywhere."

"Are you keeping it clean?" Sylvie asked me.

"It's clean, just crowded."

"Let me have a look." She swept past me up the stairs, crossing the threshold of our former home sweet home for the first time in months.

You know how it works right? How when someone else looks at something it changes the way you see it, because you're seeing it through their eyes? Suddenly it did look a little untidy, a little neglected—the living room was strewn with newspapers and magazines left open and old coffee cups and a few cereal bowls with an eighth of an inch of milk gone hard in the bottom. In the kitchen a clutter of crusty-looking dishes pretty much filled the sink, and the overflow competed for counter space with dirty pots and pans, various boxes and cans of food, breads and cereals and even potatoes and onions, and things that should have been refrigerated like hummus and half-chopped cucumbers.

"Do you not put anything away, ever?" Sylvie said.

"I like to be able to see what's available to eat," I said. "If I don't see it, I don't think to eat it."

"Why is the granola like that?"

A granola box on the counter was its normal rectangular self at the base, but at the top end the cardboard had been stretched into a circular shape, an oval, as if I'd pushed my face in there and eaten straight from the box. In fact that's exactly what I'd done. Yes, I'd been caught out. I'd grazed, handless, like a dog or cat. Under Sylvie's accusatory gaze I could feel myself blushing.

"You ate it right out of the box, didn't you?"

"There were no clean bowls or spoons," I said. I felt wrongly indicted. There was no crime committed here. Who needs cultural contrivances like bowls and spoons when the food is already in a package that can be lifted to your face????

"Trevor, I'm beginning to wonder about you," Sylvie said. She said it with such caring sympathy that I remembered what she used to be like, how she used to care for me. She brought a hand up to touch my face, looking into my eyes questioningly, disquietedly, as if the withdrawal of her love had reduced me to this—I was a nutbar who shoved my face into granola boxes like a horse with a bag of oats.

My jaw kick-started into a serious throb just now, just as I wrote that phrase down: the withdrawal of her love. My jaw has been killing me lately, as you know. Plus I'm itchy. I have clusters of little spots on my torso and I'm starting to think hair might be sprouting from them because of how rough it feels. Weird. Here I am in bed scribbling into my notebook. I should've gotten one that comes with a lock and key—wouldn't want the kids to find this and read it—if you do find this, Melissa, I don't really think you're a bad kid and I love you. If it's Kyle reading this, well son, I'm your dad, so I love you unconditionally, but the jury is out on whether I *like* you, especially after the spectacular tantrum you pulled this evening, and I'm not sorry I called you a "fucking ingrate" and a "nasty little shit." I shouldn't have sworn but it felt good and right and justified at the time and even now it feels true.

We got off on the wrong foot this evening and never got back in balance. Here I'd been so excited, just quaking with eagerness when they first arrived to tell them all about Primula, the little glistening newborn beauty in the back yard, but the moment to tell them about Primula never came—I couldn't coax the two of them into an open, friendly, family-feeling psychological mood where we were all getting along. I couldn't risk Kyle snarling "Who gives a crap?" or some other such blaspheme back at me. These days no one gets under my skin like Kyle. Right now the kids are finally in bed and settled; all the tension and petty dislike that filled the house all evening has dissipated into the quiet deep sleep of childhood, and I feel this tremendous longing to head out to the back yard and bed down in the open air. But I can't, I have to stay in, I need to be in the house because if there's a fire or anything, their mother will kill me if they get incinerated while I snooze under the stars.

Their mother. Sylvie. She seemed so concerned for me just as she was leaving, standing in the doorway of Gordon's Head, this house that used to be our happy home. I had this odd idea, not so much an idea as a *want*: I wanted to step out the door, circle behind her, put my head between her shoulder blades, and gently but insistently push her toward the threshold of the house, until she had no choice but to step inside. Then I'd slam the door and steer her to the bedroom which she would allow me to do quite willingly, and it'd all be grand and glorious again like honeymoon days and I'd keep her here forever.

Just a fantasy. Because too much has happened. Impossible to turn back time, as the Backstreet Boys used to croon. That song's like what... twenty-five years old already? They must be old and jowly by now. Hope so. They were vain fuckers in their youth.

Between my jaw aching and being required to sleep indoors I slept poorly last night. I cannot believe I ever thought sleeping anywhere but outside is a normal way to behave. Sleeping indoors sucks! It's so fucking claustrophobic! You are trapped in a room, utterly removed from what's really going on around you—if you hear some unknown person, or dog, or cat or raccoon or deer outside, you can't just lift your head and see who it is, or check out what they're up to. You have to get up out of bed and open a curtain and look out a window, and by then it's all moved on and you missed it. I can't do that anymore! I need to know what's going on. I need to check in with the girls, especially Charlene, and make sure Primula is okay.

This morning I got up before the kids and went out to see the girls, but I couldn't find them. That's unsettling. I came back and the kids were up and getting cereal by themselves in the kitchen I'd spent late-night hours cleaning, and sleep had put them in a better mood so I told them about Charlene giving birth to Primula.

"There's a baby fawn right out back?" Kyle asked. He sounded pretty thrilled.

"Yeah, isn't that cool?"

"It's happened before, like, every year," said Melissa. "How come you're making such a big deal out of this one?"

"It's true, come spring there's a new crop of fawns around the neighbourhood. But since you guys moved out I've had more time on my hands, so I've gotten to know the girls better. I feel part of it, like an uncle or something."

"The *funny* uncle," said Melissa.

"Stop it," I said. "You don't even know what that means. I hope."

"Can we catch it?" Kyle asked.

"No we cannot catch it. Why would you want to catch it?"

"So we can pet it—like the baby goats at Beacon Hill Park—only this one would be our own special private one we wouldn't have to share with anyone else."

"Those goats at the Petting Zoo are super dusty, and they poop everywhere, and there's a million little kids chasing them around," Melissa said. "I hate that place."

"You used to love it."

"When I was little, which I'm no longer."

"You used to be fearless, before your mother made you all paranoid about dust and dirt, and poop. You're introverted enough as it is."

"Nobody loves those things except animals. Pigs especially. I'm a human."

"Yeah, you're just so much above it, aren't you?"

"I want to catch the fawn!" Kyle said.

"No catching. Looking but no touching. It might be hard to find her, anyway. I couldn't find her this morning. Charlene hides Primula when she goes off to forage."

"Porridge?"

"Not porridge, idiot, forage," said Melissa. "It means to look for something to eat. Like grasses and leaves and fruits and stuff."

"Forridge for porridge!"

"Shut up."

"Let's go look for the fawn!" Kyle shouted.

After breakfast we headed out to the back yard. Kyle was diverted by the flattened patches in the long grass where the girls like to bed down—he ran from one to the next, throwing himself down in each and shouting, "You can't even see me, can you?"

"Barely," I said.

Then single file we took the narrow path into the thicket.

"Here Primula," Melissa cooed. "Come on out girl."

"She's not going to come," I said. "She's conditioned by instinct to lie stock-still when anything's coming. The white spots fawns have on their coats add camouflage, so it's almost impossible to find her. You can't see her, you can't hear her, and you can't even smell her— once her mother licks her clean, a little baby fawn has no smell."

"What about if she poops?" asked Kyle. "That would smell."

"That's true. Good point. Actually, when she poops her mother eats it up as it comes out."

"She puts her mouth right to its butt?" Kyle asked, incredulous.

"That is so gross!" said Melissa.

"No it's not, not really. All the fawn eats at this stage is mother's milk, so what comes out is nothing more than mother's milk that's been semi-digested. It probably tastes like cottage cheese."

"Cottage cheese from her butt hole!" Kyle shouted.

"Shhh! Keep looking for her, she's back here somewhere I'm pretty sure."

"This is where ticks live," said Melissa.

"Stop obsessing over ticks! There are no ticks."

"Something bit me!"

"A mosquito. Ticks don't bite like that. You don't feel them. They latch on and suck your blood for a couple of days before they let go."

"Disgusting! I'm going back inside."

"Relax, sweetie. Please. It's beautiful back here." We were beyond the filtered shade of the Garry Oaks, back where a couple of scrub alder spread a canopy that direct sunlight can't penetrate. It was cool enough in the shade to raise goose bumps on my bare arms.

"I think I see something," said Kyle excitedly.

"Like what?"

"It's a deer. Over here!" The main path was only as wide as his hips, but he veered off it onto an even tinier tributary that slit into snowberry bushes with new leaves unfurling amid shrivelled remnants of white berries from last fall. I was worried he was going to scratch his eyes on the latticework of small branches, and called out "Be careful there," and— well, just at that moment came the shock of his life—we all were shocked—as Charlene herself, a full-grown female Columbian black-tailed deer, came charging at him, her head lowered, butting him in the chest and knocking him backwards on his ass. She stood over him for just a second, looking like she might lift her front legs and commence to trampling him with her pointy black hooves. I shouted "Back off!" at her, the first time I'd ever raised my voice in anger against her. She lifted her head to look at me and amplified her nostrils so wide they looked like black tunnels running all the way to her brain. She snorted a strange sucking sound through them, protesting against our trespass, and for just a second her eyes fixed me with a look that cut me to the bone. Her look said, "You're a traitor, Trevor." Then with a sudden bound and two leaps, she shot past me and Melissa, darted right between us, moving with speed and adrenalin that human beings have forgotten exists.

Nature is scary, and sudden, and shocking. It raises the blood and the pulse. That's as frightened as I've been in a long time. Scared half to death by a deer, a herbivore. What would it do to me to come face to face with a cougar, or a bear, or a wolf—head to head with a carnivore choosing fight over flight? Charlene was in flight—she zipped past us to the side of the house, heading around front, but she stopped at the corner to look back, tempting us to chase after her, to divert us from wherever Primula was hiding, maybe? Kyle was still down on the ground, howling his lungs out. Melissa was in shock, muttering Oh My God over and over like a pre-teen robot, then bursting into tears and running to the back door.

I tried to sit Kyle up, but he was having none of it. He kept right on howling. Sometimes kids have to cry it out, and this was one of those times. Eventually the howls turned to sobs, the sobs turned to whimpers, the whimpers turned to sniffles, and at last he sat up and wiped his teary eyes with his forearm. Then he noticed something on his arm.

"He bit me!" he cried.

"He did not bite you. And it's a she by the way."

"Lookit! It bit me on the arm!"

"She. She did not. I saw the whole thing."

He held out his bare forearm to show me. It did look like teeth marks. Two rows, like bottom teeth and top teeth—on the top row were faint marks and one more serious-looking indent that had drawn a pinprick of blood. On the bottom row the marks were super-faint.

"It's not a bite. It's just the way you fell."

"It's a bite! I put my hand up like this to block it when it bashed me, and it bit me."

"I think she just butted you and knocked you down."

"I'm not lying!"

"Okay, okay. Let's go inside, clean you up a little, and have a better look at it."

He let me lift him from sitting to standing, and I brushed him off a bit, and we headed toward the back door. Charlene was long gone. From the side of the house I heard a voice call out, "Is everything all right over there?"

It was Klara, from next door, right up against the fence.

"Everything's fine," I said.

"A deer bit me!" Kyle yelled.

Jesus Christ.

"What? Where? Are you all right?"

The offer of comfort in her voice was like a siren's call to the kid, and he beelined to her, holding his arm high. "Right here! Right here, look!"

By the time I got over there, Klara was in full-on alarmist mode. "Those are definitely teeth marks. This is serious—you're going to need a tetanus shot at the very least, or maybe even rabies—"

"Don't start with rabies," I said. "Tetanus, I'm pretty sure all his shots are up to date."

"Well you better make sure. Does it hurt?"

"A little bit."

"Do you have Polysporin at home?"

Kyle looked up at me expectantly.

"I'm pretty sure we do."

"If you don't, I do," said Klara. "Are you going to call Sylvie?"

"What for?"

"To see if his shots are up to date."

"I don't want to worry her for nothing."

"Trevor, this is serious! She needs to know. If you don't call her I will."

"I'll call her. I'll call her."

Jesus Christ.

We went back in the house. Melissa was upstairs looking out the living room window. "A deer is just hanging around in the front yard," she said. "Is it the same one?"

"Yeah, that's Charlene," I said. "She's worried about her baby. We spooked her. I'm sure she doesn't like being separated. I'm sure she's quite upset."

"Are you going to put Polysporin on?" Kyle asked. "That deer bit me!" He held out his forearm to his sister, who for once showed an interest in him.

"It did?"

"Yeah, look. It made teeth marks."

"Maybe," I said.

"Klara said it did for sure!"

"Klara is not an expert."

"She said to phone mommy."

"I will text mommy."

"Right now."

"Right now."

I found some antiseptic ointment in the bathroom and slathered it on Kyle's arm and then, with the children's eyes upon me, I let my finger hover over the phone until my mind had decided on the following statement of fact:

We were out back and spooked a deer.

Charlene, it was.

She might have nipped at Kyle.

He's all right now.

I pressed Send. It took about thirty seconds for the phone to ring.

"You got my text?" I asked.

"Yes. I already knew because Klara texted me."

Jesus Christ.

We talked for about three minutes. It was determined that while Kyle was supposed to have gotten a tetanus booster in grade one, in the upheaval of the end of our marriage this small but important detail had been overlooked.

So. Off we went to spend Saturday morning and into the afternoon at the emergency ward of Vic General, passing the hours on easily wipeable plastic chairs amidst a whole herd of people suffering misery worse than ours. Kyle was happily oblivious to the sickness and despair—I let him bring his iPad and told him he could play *Kingdom Rush* until his brain turned to porridge. Eventually a nice young doctor with a trace of a Slavic accent looked at the marks on his arm. We decided it wasn't a bite, *per se*—the marks were too minor to be from teeth clamping down hard, and therefore most likely they were caused by the momentary collision of deer teeth against boy flesh as Charlene bolted past him. I was happy with that diagnosis. The young doctor excused himself to google deer bites in the corner of the examination room, and complained that because ticks are called "deer ticks" he couldn't google deer bites without getting the results for deer tick bites. I never said the word "rabies" and neither did he; I was happy when he said a tetanus booster would suffice. He said we were the second deer-related incident he'd treated this week—an old lady had been knocked on her ass while walking her little white Pomeranian, and the deer had tried to trample the dog. "The poor old girl broke her hip in the fall, but she was more worried about the doggie, because apparently deer hooves are sharp as knives" he said. "It made the local news, did you see it? It's the time of year, apparently—does are birthing fawns and get very protective of them. Funny, isn't it? You'd think it would be males we'd worry about. They're bigger, and they have those horns."

"Antlers, not horns," I corrected him. "Horns continue to grow for the life of the animal, antlers fall off and are replaced every year."

He looked at me funny. "Anyhow, this time of year males make themselves scarce," I said. "They really only show themselves in October, November, for the rut. That's when they go from being hermits to horndogs overnight—one of them this past fall spent weeks stalking the girls, crisscrossing my property with a hard on."

"The girls?"

"Yeah. Three does that live with me. Marlene, Darlene, and Charlene. Charlene's the one who ran over Kyle. The three of them bed down in back of my house."

"You're a deer aficionado," he said. Mockery in his tone, just a smidgen. I don't know why I was babbling but I couldn't seem to stop.

"Yeah, I called that buck Bruno, he used to give me the evil eye sometimes. I used to trail around after him, at a distance, because I'd been reading up on their courtship rituals, and I wanted to witness it for myself. First of all, the male needs to coax the female to urinate, but he averts his eyes while she does it, which is very gentlemanly I think—and then she moves off and he goes to the urine-soaked spot of ground or grass or whatever, and does this thing with his mouth where he curls his upper lip up and over his nose, which exposes his Jacobson's organ—have you heard of that? It's a special smell-sorting organ deer have, and within a few seconds of sniffing and licking he can tell if she's in heat or not! Wild, eh? It's like special powers—supernatural powers that we can't even conceive of!"

The doctor smiled a patronizing little smile at me, and said, "Cool."

That was all the encouragement I needed to keep right on babbling. "I saw Bruno do that once with Charlene. He must have liked what he smelled, because he came up behind her and let out this high-pitched moaning sound that is apparently close to the distress call of a fawn—that's the seduction technique, the doe hears what sounds to her like a fawn in distress and that triggers all kinds of maternal hormones, and she turns and sees the male near her butt with his head held low, making a big-eyed cutesy needy fawn face, so that melts her heart even more, and then she notices he's got a big thick-necked male body, and impressive antlers, and that gives her another kind of thrill, and she's ready for action! Only in this case Charlene wasn't ready—she ran off, out the back of my thicket into Mount Doug Park, cause my property backs onto Mount Doug Park. I was going to chase after them and keep watching but I didn't. I thought maybe she ran off 'cause she wanted privacy. So I don't know if she let him have his way with her or not. He used to chase all three of the girls around, but so far it seems like only Charlene got impregnated. A doe can get pregnant as young as seven months, but more often they're sexually mature at eighteen months, so either Marlene and Darlene are still carrying fawns and haven't dropped yet, or they're late bloomers and weren't ready to get pregnant this year. They're only a year old."

At this point Kyle interrupted to whine, "Can we go?" For some reason this irritated the hell out of me—I could feel my nostrils stretch wide as I sucked in air, and I shouted "Yes!" at him, all out of proportion to the situation, and even made a gesture toward him, a kind of single high-stepping strut in his direction, like I wanted to trample him or something. This prompted the doc to ask if I was all right.

"I'm fine," I insisted. "The only problem I have is my jaw is killing me."

"I noticed you pushing your bottom teeth out and biting your upper lip."

"I do it without thinking. It feels better."

"It looks weird," Kyle said.

"Shut up."

"Can we *please* go?"

"I'm just going to have a look at you for a minute," said the doctor. He put his hands to my jaw and felt my glands on each side. I had to fight the urge to twist away, like a horse that hates the bridle. "Your jaw is swollen a little. Open wide." He shone a light in my throat. "Do you have your wisdom teeth?"

"No. They were pulled years ago. I'm forty-nine years old."

"It almost looks like a new set of teeth are coming in back there. Big ones, just getting set to break the skin. If I were you, I'd go see a dentist first chance you get."

"I'm also itchy," I said.

"Mild or severe?"

"Not severe. But noticeable."

"A mild itch is not something we deal with in the ER."

took Kyle to Michael's waterfront mansion, which over-
looks Haro Strait off of Arbutus Road. You drive down
to it through big Douglas fir trees that must be four hundred
years old, on a single-lane driveway so narrow in spots it
feels like those ancient trunks will scrape a side mirror off
your car. The ride's bumpy because the roots of the trees run
like underground knuckles lifting and cracking the asphalt.
Then the trees give way to a vast lawn mowed all criss-
cross so it looks like plaid, and the road circles by the front
door. All very grand and intimidating. I hate going there— it
reminds me I'll never get close to that kind of money. Alpha-
male money. I punch a clock for chump change and a measly
pension. No one to blame for that but myself, though. Land
of opportunity but I didn't seize the day.

Anyhow, I brought Kyle to the door and he tried to open
it but it was locked, so I rang the bell and in a minute the
door was swung open by a woman I've never seen in my
life. She was young, probably like 22, and pretty, I should
say more than pretty, because now that I've reached the ripe
and rotting age of 49, every 20-something female on the
planet looks pretty damn fine. They still have their youth,
and "youth is beauty," right? Keats, right? Or was it truth?
Should have been youth. Youth is beauty, beauty youth.
Anyway this lovely young thing was a bit on the chunky

side but still fit, with sturdy tanned legs descending from short shorts. She spoke in a Scandinavian accent, showing a symmetrical white smile that probably cost her parents high four figures at an Oslo orthodontist's. She said "Hi" to Kyle in a very familiar way, then said, "You must be Trevor," and looked me in the eye with just a hint of pity. That gleam in her eye said, *Sylvie's told me the whole story, you poor thing, you poor loser.* Or maybe I was reading too much into it. I was off-kilter to begin with. Maybe that look of hers was just the standard default of merry bemusement Scandinavian girls present to the world—all those lovely butterflies emerging with perfect hair and teeth from their cocoon of the best social safety net on the planet. Lucky girls.

Kyle darted through the door and disappeared inside, and before I could say a word Melissa came bounding up—Sylvie had picked her up from Gordon's Head while Kyle and I were at Emergency—and said, "Did you bring his homework and piano book?" No smile. No welcome. Surly little bitch.

"No I didn't."

"Mom texted you."

"I did not see it."

"She's going to be pissed."

"You're eleven. Don't use that word."

"*Pissed.* Royally pissed."

Kyle had found Michael, his soon-to-be official step-dad, in some nearby inner room, where I could hear him spitting out in rapid little kid-bursts the whole adventure of being "attacked" by Charlene, who "wanted to kill" him.

"It wasn't like that, guys," I yelled over Melissa's head.

Meanwhile Sylvie came pitter-pattering down the massive sweeping staircase that dominates the foyer—everything in that house is oversized and pretentious as hell—and started grilling me on what the doctor said. The Scandinavian girl was still standing there, taking it all in.

"We haven't been introduced," I said.

"This is Birgitta. She's from Copenhagen."

"Nice to meet you," said Birgitta.

"She's our *au pair*," said Melissa happily, like *"au pair"* was the coolest, most exotic term in the whole world.

"Bully for you," I told her. To Sylvie I said, "Now you need a servant?"

"Not a servant, an *au pair*. And yes, Michael thought so. We have a lot of functions in the evenings—social events, charity balls—the calendar is crowded. It's a couple's world. He needs me on his arm."

"He's a mover and shaker," I said. It sounded more bitter than I intended. "The kids are bit old for an 'au pair,' aren't they? Mel is almost twelve—that's when you go from needing a babysitter to being one."

"Michael always had *au pairs* with his own kids. It's just easier. Now tell me more about the doctor."

I proceeded to lay it out pretty much exactly as it went down, until she got irritated and interrupted me by almost shouting, "Don't downplay everything!"

"I'm not."

"You're making it sound trivial."

"Listen to the kid," I said. We could hear Kyle and Michael yukking it up in the next room. "He's treating it like a big adventure. He's not traumatized."

"We'll see how he sleeps tonight."

"Anyway, he's had his shot for tetanus, which came with boosters for diphtheria, polio, and one more—whooping cough, I think. He's up to date. So some good came out of it."

"Klara told me she phoned Saanich Animal Control."

"What for?"

"What for? A wild animal bit our child, Trevor!"

"Charlene. Protecting a tiny baby fawn."

We locked eyes in a stare down. "Whose side are you on here?" she said.

"I'm not on anybody's side. I'm on nature's side."

"Well I'm on the kids' side. And if they're at risk of being attacked by nature when they're at your place, they're staying here from now on."

"They're not going to like that," I said. "Melissa, do you like that?"

"I'm fine with that," she said. It was like a dagger to the heart.

I still hadn't crossed the threshold, I was outside in the cool air, and they were inside in the warmth of electricity and civilization, standing together shoulder to shoulder, indoor creatures rejecting the outdoor creature. I wanted my offspring to come out, to join me in the real world, the natural world. Come out, come out! Isn't that only natural?

Unfortunately I didn't express these sentiments clearly or calmly, I acknowledge that in hindsight. I raised my voice. I stamped my feet in frustration in a manner outside the range of polite human discourse. I don't know if I've stamped my feet like that ever before, it felt a bit weird even as I did it, and the words coming out of my mouth were also a bit extreme. I used inappropriate language, and when Michael emerged to stand shoulder to shoulder to shoulder with the females, and step forward a little ahead of them as if they were in danger, and told me the words I used had crossed a line, I told him the kids were my offspring, not his. I told him to Fuck. Right. Off. And Mind His Own Business.

He remained cool and level-headed, the fucker, which only maddened me more. He said, "I don't like where this is going, so I'm going to close the door now, and we'll talk about it tomorrow. Everyone's a little on edge today, not least Kyle and Melissa, after the incident they've been through. Not least you, as well—ER rooms are stressful places and you were there a long time today. Go home and have a bath. Put some Epsom salts in it. Goodbye Trevor." Then he took hold of the door, this one-of-a-kind massive cedar barrier carved at great expense in a west coast First Nations style, and he gently but resolutely began to close it, so that one after another I saw their faces disappear—first stone-faced Melissa, then Sylvie with a glimmer of compassion in her eyes, then Kyle poking his head between the grown-ups' hips, looking perplexed and distraught, then further back wide-eyed Birgitta, latest edition to Michael's fucking harem. And finally Michael himself, front and center, puffed up and self-righteous until the very end.

The door was closed. The lock clicked.

I regret what I did next, but it felt right at the time. It felt so primeval, so palpably right. I was running on instinct, you see. I kicked the door. Not once, or twice, but many times, as hard as I could.

Then I stopped and listened. Michael said, "Go home now, Trevor."

Then I heard Birgitta say, as if some local custom needed explaining, "Why is he doing this?"

Michael said, "It's nothing. Just acting weird."

That *really* put me over the edge. Instinct again. I leaned forward and butted that hand-carved artisanal door with my head, hard as I could. I wish I could say it felt deliciously right, but in the carving of the door there was an image of an otter, or a seal, a marine mammal lying belly up. In the belly-button of that animal, right at the level of my forehead as I leaned forward and lowered my head, was a little glass spy-hole for those inside to look outside. The spyhole was encircled by a brass ring that protruded slightly, so when I bashed my head against it, it punched a circle with the circumference of a nickel into the skin of my forehead.

Foreheads bleed a lot when they are cut like that. Blood was trickling—gushing—down into my eyes, and when I wiped at it with the back of my hand some of it splattered down onto the perfectly placed oversized welcome mat of their perfect fucking upper-crust home. I let it drip, tilting my head to let more blood splatter onto the concrete around the mat, thinking vengefully that blood on the floor would be much harder to deny or remove than blood on a disposable welcome mat.

That felt great. That was like marking my fucking territory. War! *Waaaaaarrrr!*

Then I heard Sylvie through the door. "Trevor, are you all right?" She was watching me through the spyhole, I intuited. Watching the blood gush.

I didn't want her sympathy. Suddenly I felt ridiculous and self-conscious, and I had the urge to flee. So I did. I just turned tail and ran. Behind me I could hear the door open, and heard Sylvie call my name, heard Melissa yell, "Ooooh gross!" at the sight of blood on the ground. Then Sylvie yelled my name more plaintively, like she really cared, and that just spurred me to get away faster. I got in the car and drove like a madman bouncing over the tree roots until I was down the long driveway and into the street a good way distant. Then I slowed and felt around on the floor for a rag I use to wipe condensation from the inside of the windshield, and I held it to my forehead to sop up the blood. I held it there all the way home.

I like it when the kids are gone. I can sleep outside. Last night I slept well and deeply; by the time my eyelids fluttered open the sun was up and warm. Really, it felt like the first day of summer. Darlene and Marlene were hunkered down in the grass twenty feet away, ten feet from each other. Funny how they sleep, if you can call it sleep—eyes closed but ears twitching on high alert. They're prey animals. They can't relax. When they sit together there's a hierarchy. Charlene as the mom is the alpha of the pack, and in deer etiquette that means she is free to sit facing the others, and to look at them, but the others have to sit in such a way that they're not looking at her face. That's rude. Apparently all ruminants do this—next time you drive by some cows sitting in a field, note how they're all sitting so none of them is looking into the face of another.

Anyway, it seemed to me that in Charlene's absence I was top dog, because Marlene and Darlene were seated so as to avoid looking directly at me. Or maybe they thought of me as their equal, and were unnerved and offended that I was breaking protocol by looking right at them in oblivious human klutziness. Or maybe they thought I looked weird with that third eye on my forehead. I ran a fingertip around it. It had a scab which felt kind of tenuous, like I could flick it off with a fingernail. What can you do? The sun felt good. "Hey guys," I said. "Where's Charlene and the baby?" I got up and stretched, and that was their cue to get up too. They did their leisurely, unstressed rise to a standing position, which is strange to watch because it looks so tortuous and graceless—they roll from their side onto their belly, then heave up awkwardly onto their front knees, then pitch their weight forward while they untuck their hindquarters and straighten out their hind legs. Then they extend one of their front legs, and lift the body so the other front leg can slip forward and find footing, kind of like if a human were to plant both feet on the ground and straighten out their legs before getting up off their elbows. With all four feet on *terra firma*, the two girls stretched out, lazily as a yawn, and sauntered off. I should note here that this is their slow, casual way of getting up. They also have a quick way when startled or frightened: They tuck all four legs under themselves and then pop!—in an instant they explode onto four feet and are gone. I used to see that a lot, before they got used to me.

I was heading inside to make a cup of coffee when my peripheral vision caught a quicksilver movement in Jim and Klara's back yard.

It was Primula, darting back and forth behind the chain link fence, looking a bit frantic. The three-foot fence was too tall for her to jump clear. "Hey little one," I called. "How'd you get in there?" I went around the side of their house to open their gate, to shoo her back into my yard. It felt a bit funny trespassing onto Jim and Klara's private property—

they don't take kindly to uninvited people compressing their perfectly manicured grass—but I had to do it. That's when I heard Klara call from her kitchen window.

"What's going on, Trevor?"

"I'm trying to steer Primula out of here. I don't know how she got in."

She caught sight of the fawn and let out that tender, motherly "*Awwww!*" women make when they see a baby deer. I'm not knocking or mocking women for it, because it's totally justified—fawns are about the cutest little babies on the planet.

Primula pranced off into the furthest corner of the yard, painting herself into a corner. As I came closer she gave a nervous shiver and suddenly darted head-first through a three-inch gap where the side and back fences meet. It was unbelievable that she could even squeeze through there—she lowered her head like a battering ram and charged at it, bashing her skull against the two fence poles, which made a sound like a puck clanging off a cross bar. Ouch. The sound lingered longer than the sight of her; she vanished into the dense brush of my unkempt back forty.

Klara came out of her house. "Where'd she go?" she said.

"She's back in my thicket. She slipped through that gap there."

"No she couldn't."

"She could. She did."

"She's awfully cute."

"Yeah. No wonder her mother's so protective."

"I think you know I called Saanich Animal Control?"

"That wasn't necessary."

"They said they'd be by this morning."

"Why did you do that, anyway?"

"The deer bit a child, Trevor."

Jesus Christ.

"Protecting her baby," I said.

Jim came out and joined us.

"What happened to your forehead?" he said.

"I bashed it against something."

"It's like a third eye, centered like that. Perfect circle, like a ring. Looks like Sylvie gave her wedding ring back—with a hammer." I felt hairs go erect on the back of my neck. In fact all over my body. Like an angry itch.

"Jim!" said Klara. "Don't be a jerk."

"Well it does," he said. "Hey Trevor, did you hear about the new bylaw? Property owners are about to get the right to cull nuisance deer!"

"Cull? Like kill? You want to kill Primula?"

"She's a nuisance, the little rascal," said Klara. "I don't care how cute she is, I don't want her in my yard. I won't even feel safe if I see her, knowing the mother might attack me."

"I'll tie a two-by-four in that gap. That'll keep her out. She's too young to jump the fence."

"It's the bigger ones that get my goat." Klara was looking over my shoulder at Darlene and Marlene, who were sauntering from the street into my back yard again.

"Those two I'd love to get culled," said Jim. "I'm going to ask The Pound about that when they come by."

"Here's your chance," I said.

Between the houses we could see a white pickup slowing on the street. It had cages in the bed and had Saanich Animal Control written on the side. Probably it reeked of miscreant dogs, because Darlene and Marlene took one sniff and high-tailed it back into my thicket.

"The deer know!" Jim crowed. "You can run but you can't hide!"

The Animal Control Officer was about what you'd expect—a brawny guy, Mike, who looked like he could wrestle alligators. He gave off the animal-friendly vibe of a rescuer, not a culler. Klara had placed the call that brought him, but since I was the one who'd witnessed "the incident," he was more interested in my story. While I laid it out, Klara only interrupted once, to say, "The boy was in shock!"

"He wasn't," I said. "Afterwards he made it sound like a big adventure."

"That's not what Sylvie told me!"

Mike said Kyle was lucky he hadn't been sliced and diced while he was lying defenceless on the ground. "A doe in that situation will sometimes kick like crazy, and their hooves are sharp enough to disembowel a dog," he said. "I've seen it."

Klara shivered. "That doesn't make me feel safe."

"Charlene would not do that, though," I said. "She had a chance, but she didn't do it."

"It's not often people know deer by name," said Mike.

"Yeah well, I've got three does that live in back, plus a fawn. It's like base camp for them to forage the neighbourhood. I've spent enough time with them I can tell them apart. Tell their personalities. The fawn's name is Primula."

"Nice," said Mike. I can say I liked Mike. He seemed to be on my side.

Klara said, "Razor sharp hooves and they're so crazy to protect their fawns—it's just like getting caught between a momma grizzly and her cubs! It could be deadly dangerous! Can't something be done?"

"Culled," said Jim. "I vote for culled."

"Looks like Council's going to pass a law about that," said Mike. "They're voting on it tonight. But as it stands they're protected under the Wildlife Act and I can't interfere with them. That's a job for the Provincial Conservation Officers. They might step in if the deer is threatening pets or people repeatedly, but this seems an isolated case, a cornered animal panicking."

"What exactly do you do, then?" asked Jim. His tone was like, *What the hell are you good for, anyway?* But Mike stayed cool. Mike *was* cool.

"When it comes to deer, we're mostly picking up dead ones," he said. "Hundreds die each year in Saanich alone, if you can believe that. Mostly hit by cars."

"Really? The way they cross the road around here, they're super careful," I said. "One step, look both ways, chew some cud; another step, look both ways, chew some cud. It takes them forever just to cross the street."

"I know it. The more urban the area, the more savvy they are. But if they're spooked, or if they live in the less-populated farmland areas, they're not as wise to it. Even around here, if they're spooked, or chased by a dog, they'll dart out into traffic."

"The fawns don't know any better than to run willy-nilly into the road, so a lot of them must get killed that way," I said. "I worry about that."

"Actually a lot of fawns are poisoned," said Mike. "They don't know not to eat foxglove, which is loaded up with digitoxins that are deadly to deer. Deadly to humans too."

"I'm planting some foxglove, then," said Jim. "Gonna be a freaking foxglove plantation around here!"

"Shut up," I said.

"Don't tell me what to do on my own property, Trevor. And why are you scratching like that?"

"I'm itchy." I had my hand under my shirt, clawing at stubble.

Mike had one of those walkie-talkie type things on his chest like cops wear, and it erupted in a static-thick message about a pair of pit bull crosses on the loose in Cadboro Bay. "I gotta run," he said. "Thanks for taking the time to call. Let us know if there are any more incidents."

As we watched him run off to his truck I felt good—vindicated. Jim and Klara were feeling the opposite. "What a complete waste of taxpayer dollars," Jim said.

"He cleans up hundreds of dead deer a year," I said. "Plus he's just gone off to corral some pit bulls. You call that a waste of money? I'm glad he's around. Now if you'll excuse me I'll fix that gap in your fence so Primula won't ever bother you."

"You treat those deer better than your own kids," Jim said.

"They treat me better too. They're not as lippy."

n my workshop in the basement I rooted around until I found a two-by-four of appropriate length, drilled a couple of holes in it, found some wire, and tied it in that gap in the fence. When I was done I took a stroll back into the deeper woods to see if I could spot Primula. If I could just see her, know where she was, and be sure she hadn't done damage to her skull crashing between those fence posts, it would settle my mind. Jim was right in a way—I felt very protective of Primula. You'd think she was mine or something. I caught glimpses of her moving around through the brush, skipping and charging about in a happy dance. So pure, so naive. Uncorrupted.

I kept my distance, and when I turned to leave there was Charlene. She'd been behind me, watching me the way I'd been watching Primula. She didn't seem bothered by me, and I had no worries that she might try to trample me with razor-sharp hooves.

"There you are," I said softly. "Your daughter went looking for you and got in a whole bunch of trouble next door."

She stood blocking the narrow path that was my exit route back to the house. I started walking toward her but she made no move to accommodate my passing. "I'll leave you to her," I said. Then she did a funny thing—she shifted her weight forward to her front legs and brought her hind legs close together so that she looked kind of knock-kneed. She rubbed her legs together at the hocks, and then, to my complete surprise, a stream of urine came down from under her belly and landed on her hocks. Man-oh-man—talk about a pungent smell! Just about knocked me over, the smell of it! It was trippy. I felt weird, like I'd inhaled some new mind-altering, dodgy drug. Like, hey, this is getting me really, really high, but is it something I can handle?

Everyone knows that when animals meet and greet they sniff each other to check each other out, right? Dogs take a good whiff of butts, we've all seen that. Well, when deer get together they check out each other's hocks. They'll pee often on their own hocks through the day, and then lick them to take the edge off, until they convey just the right scented representation of who they are, or who they want the world to think they are, and then when they meet another deer they'll lick and smell that deer's hocks, and vice versa, and it'll be like, *Hey girl, you are smelling great—you must be eating some top grade alfalfa and getting a good night's sleep these days!* Or maybe, *Hey, have you been super-stressed lately? What's up with that?*

Deer have weird glands in weird places. They have glands called "interdigital glands" between their toes—interdigital, like between digits, right?—and these glands leave a tiny bit of scent on the ground with every step, which helps other deer track them around, especially bucks tracking females during the rut. They also have glands in other places too, but the most important glands are the tarsals, on the hocks, the ones Charlene was freshening up for me. The secretions of sudoriferous glands under the skin are carried to the surface by hair follicles. "Sudoriferous" is a word you've probably never heard, but I'm telling you—Charlene's smell as she peed on herself was the most amazing fragrance that ever went up my nose in my whole entire life! "Fragrance" doesn't do it justice! "Fragrance" makes it sound like I untwisted the lid of a bottle of eau de cologne or something—this was like the whole fucking perfume factory got crammed up my nose and blew my brains out my ears! It got me sloppy drunk and dizzy and I almost stumbled as I tried to pass her on that narrow path. She did not step aside for me. What she did was lower her head as if she wanted to smell *my* hocks as I passed, and so I stopped to let her, and in my dizziness put a hand on her back to steady myself. I touched her and felt a jolt, like some severe, unspeakable taboo had been broken. In an instant she bolted; she was gone like a rocket down the path and out of sight into the thicket. All I could do was call after her, "Sorry, Charlene." *Damn. Shouldn't have touched her!*

The spell had been broken, and I felt shame and regret. Never touch each other when you're sniffing tarsals, idiot!

"Touched her and felt a jolt—like some severe, unspeakable taboo had been broken. In an instant she bolted; she was gone like a rocket down the path and out of sight into the thicket."

I was reading this out loud to Rolanda. Rolanda's why I'm writing all this down in the first place, remember? She suggested I bring my journal to our sessions and if I felt up to it read some to her. The strategy is, you write down things you can't bring yourself to say, and once you've written them down, they become easier to say.

We had a session this morning. I got to book time off work for it, which is excellent. Leaving the office I felt a weight lift, felt sunlight on my face, but the closer I got to Rolanda's place, the weight came back. Do I really need to talk about crap? It's not pleasant. In fact, it's painful. That was my mindset. So we sat in silence. Seems like she wanted me to lead. My skin was itchy as hell all across my chest and back, and my jaw was acting up; I had to consciously prevent myself from doing that thing where I pull my bottom teeth out and rub my upper lip with them. Her little safe-space with the couch and cushions felt small and airless and I could feel my eyes darting all over looking for an exit. She probably saw this as evasiveness, but it was claustrophobia pure and simple—the smaller the room, the harder it is for me to be at peace.

She broke the stalemate by asking how the journal was going, and when I showed her my notebook she said, "Wow, you've been busy!" "It gives me something to do," I said, and winced in my head because it made me sound pathetic and lonely. She coaxed me to read a page or two—she said choose something that had special significance for me, and I chose my meeting with Charlene along the thicket path; for one, because it just happened yesterday and it was fresh in my mind, and for two, it had given me a restless, near-sleepless night, and when I woke up in the morning in the back yard Charlene was resting casually not ten feet from me. That was what I was keen to tell Rolanda—that Charlene had forgiven me for touching her.

I kept reading: "All I could do was call after her, 'Sorry, Charlene.' *Damn. Shouldn't have touched her!* The spell had been broken, and I felt shame and regret. Never touch each other when you're sniffing tarsals, idiot!"

I stopped there and lifted my head, looking at Rolanda expectantly. She didn't say anything at first. The wheels were turning.

"It's all about deer," she said.

"Yes. Or actually, no. Me and deer."

"I was hoping for a little bit more about *you*, though. Maybe some thoughts on your marriage, your relationship to Sylvie."

"Fuck her," I said. It surprised me. It came out like a snort, like "Fuhgger!"

"Trevor," she said. Not scolding though. Very neutral. "Why do you think you said that?"

"I don't know. It was like instinct. It felt good." Then I thought, *You know what? I would like to fuck Sylvie.* And then I thought, *I would like to fuck just about anyone... I haven't fucked anyone in sixteen months.* Then I realised I'd said both things out loud.

"Sixteen months. So since Sylvie left, you've been celibate."

"Correct."

"That's not unusual."

"I know."

"After trust has been broken."

"Uh huh."

"It's very difficult, until we heal, to be open to new relationships. Do you ever imagine yourself in a new relationship?"

"Maybe."

"Anyone in mind?"

"No."

I didn't say it, but I was thinking, *Do I have a relationship with Charlene? Would that be too weird?* Certainly too weird to say to Rolanda in her claustrophobic, overly pillowed cocoon. I kept my mouth shut.

Is it right to keep thoughts from your therapist? Earlier in our session, I'd already kept something from her, because she asked me why I had a scab-mark on my forehead in the shape of a perfect circle, and I told her I fell off my bike and hit my head on the handlebars, not the handlebar itself but something attached to it, a protruding metal circle that used to have a bell mounted on it. When I was a kid I had a bike with a bell on the handlebars, but then the bell part broke off, leaving only a circular metal base still attached. It's amazing how the brain can out of nowhere so easily fabricate an untruth using a little bit of some truthful thing remembered, and how visualizing hitting your head on that remembered thing makes it almost seem like it happened. This is what sets us apart from the animals: We are the only species that can lie. We're the crooked species. The con artists. Bullshit came out of my mouth, and even as I heard it I was asking myself internally, *Why are you being evasive here? Why keep secrets?* I'm not *totally* keeping things from Rolanda because I've already written in this journal all about whacking my skull against Michael's door, and right now I'm writing about how I tried to keep my mouth shut about my thoughts re: Charlene, and that means I might have to read them to Rolanda next time we meet, or sometime in the future. That would be good. A good way to broach it. I'll read her this and she'll know: I'm more interested in deer than humans right now. I'm not talking about sexually. Sexually I'm attracted to women, obviously. The thought of a sweet doe-eyed (Fuck!—I can't believe I said "doe-eyed," but I am talking about women here, honest, and that is a nice attribute for a woman under any circumstances, right?)... Anyhow, a sweet woman who is non-judgemental, a kind of Earth Mother type who likes sleeping outside maybe, waking with skin all fresh and cool like dew in the morning, and we'd be spooning there all night, all snuggled close and warm, and then she'd guide my hand down between her legs to let me feel her nice warm juicy pussy—these thoughts make me almost cry with longing, you get me? I would *love love love* to earn the privilege of access to some nice woman's nice warm juicy pussy right now, but I'm realistic. I'm no catch. I'm forty-fucking-nine years old, I've been tossed in the trash by the love of my life, and I'm depressed and angry and I keep acting out at work. I get that. I'm not in denial. Every human being needs love and intimacy, and not getting those things is at the root of my troubles, I know that. Not rocket science. Intimacy: When I think of where I could go to get it, another human being is way too much work. On rare good days I used to get a wee bit of tenderness, a little buzz of familial love from my own flesh and blood, Melissa and Kyle, but that seems to have gone down the shitter lately. Now they won't even be staying at the house with me anymore, seems like. Charlene is the one sentient being I feel close to right now. Deep down I truly do worry about her and Primula. I feel protective. I feel like a part of their little family.

These were the very thoughts ricocheting round my skull when Rolanda brought me back to reality. "Where are your thoughts right now?"

"You're sure you want to know?"

"Yes I do."

"I was thinking about Charlene and Primula. How we're kind of like a family."

There was a pause. "Somehow it always comes back to deer," she said.

"I know!" I said cheerfully. "I like deer a lot."

"But let's try again to talk about Sylvie."

"That's not relevant right now. I've got bigger fish to fry."

"No. Trevor, please. Focus, here. I know you care deeply about your deer friends, but that is beyond my—beyond my scope, let's say. We need to talk about human concerns. I can help you with those. I want to help you. There's a gap in my understanding of your relationship with your ex-wife, and I think we need to have a look at that. All you've shared with me so far is that you were together and happy, and then suddenly you were not together, and now you just shared that you still have feelings for her."

"I said I wanted to—well, you know what I said."

She looked at me expectantly, waiting for more.

"I don't understand women," I said. "It's like shaving without a mirror."

"Is that so hard?" she asked.

"It's annoying. Doesn't feel right."

"But it could be done, I think. Couldn't you just go by feel?"

"Try shaving your legs with your eyes closed."

"Okay. Let's keep our eyes open for now. You've never explained the process by which the two of you—"

"Split? It wasn't a process."

"Think of it as a story, then. Tell me the story. Once upon a time you were happily married. Then what happened? Or actually, let's go way back, right to the beginning—how did you two meet, and come to be together?"

"Fine. You want ancient history." Right about then I was really starting to hate that claustrophobic little room. But I sucked it up. Pulled myself together. "Pull yourself together, man!" My dad was ex-military. That was one of his pet phrases. *Pull yourself together, man.* "Once upon a time I was at work, working away at my busy little desk, the same desk I still work at to this very day, and Sylvie came into the office—she had clients upstairs, you see, patients—she worked as a community liaison nurse, which means she went out to people's houses and assessed whether or not they could function in their own home, or should be brought into a care facility like ours. I knew her name, because Mona talked to her on the phone from time to time, they were friends. But to see her in person, I was unprepared for how good-looking she was, like, gorgeous, like way out of my league, or so I thought, and also she was like, ten years younger. She'd come to see Mona—they were going out to lunch. After Mona came back I made a comment about how good-looking she was and Mona was like, 'You think so?' Her eyes went all glittery, lit up with that special scheming sparkle women get when they set themselves to matchmaking. Turns out Sylvie was newly single and I was divorced—"

"I didn't know you were married before," Rolanda interrupted.

"Okay, that's *ancient* ancient history," I said.

"Can you tell me a little bit?"

"Married at twenty-seven, divorced by thirty-one. Her name was Debra. Deb. Pretty much it came down to she wanted kids and I didn't. I can't even find my car keys, how am I supposed to keep track of a kid? That was my go-to line."

"But now you have kids."

"Exactly. How did that happen?"

She waited just the right time to say, "Well?"

"Accidents happen, right? Mona built me up to Sylvie as the nicest of guys, the perfect antidote to her previous dude, who was on the abusive side. So she gave me a try, because really who the fuck wants to be alone, and she liked me enough to let me into her bed, and probably on the second or third time we did the deed one of my squiggly little troopers overcame the battlements, and reached and breached her egg, and the rest is history. She was pro-choice, but faced with actually getting rid of something alive and growing inside her, she couldn't do it. I was infatuated, nuts about her, really, and feeling kind of proud of myself—knowing that I had given her a kid made me feel super-virile, the cock-of-the-walk. I'm like a serious person suddenly, I'm going to have a kid! Having a kid does give your life a purpose, a focus, beyond what to eat for dinner or where to vacation next winter. It was scary, but for her it was like, 'Let's dive into the future with a guy I hardly know but seems nice and comes with good references.' To me she was the brave one, I was more like the sidekick. So we went for it, and it actually worked out pretty good. We were good teammates, working together to grow our wee one. Then once you see having one doesn't kill you and actually isn't that difficult, you may as well have another one so they can keep each other company, right?"

"I suppose so," Rolanda said.

The room went quiet for a minute and I realized I had a throbbing pain near my temples, and my teeth hurt. Plus I was itchy and claustrophobic. Like a mind reader she said, "Is this difficult for you?"

"Yes. Good times long gone, you could say."

"Take your time. Breathe."

"Oh thank you." I said it too sarcastically and felt bad. Rolanda is nice, she wants to help me. Shouldn't be snarky like that. *Pull yourself together man!* I breathed, as suggested. Slowly calmed down.

"Feel better?" she said. I nodded.

"It sounds as if you two built a solid marriage."

"Correct."

Gently, delicately, she said, "And then what happened?"

"Here's the deal," I said. My head was throbbing at the temples and it made me sound curt and bitter, but there was nothing I could do. "Women are relentless improvers. They look at a perfectly comfortable, pleasant little house and can't seem to be happy with that. They're like, what if we could put in a bay window right here with nice puffy colourful throw pillows on it like in Western Living Magazine, or a sun room over here to bring more light in, or new countertops and cupboards in the kitchen even though the old ones work just fine."

"So you argued over renovations?"

"That's not the whole story. Sylvie's... She is a restless spirit, more restless than me, not satisfied with where we were in life. Two kids, manageable mortgage, nice property, woods out back—I was like, totally content with that. What more did I need? Not a thing. Sign the treaty, live in peace and relative prosperity, buy some kayaks for the weekend, it's all good. She got to the same place that made me happy, and she was like, 'Is that all there is?' She wanted more. To her I was complacent, and complacency is such a no-no these days—we're always supposed to be striving. But to me, the secret of happiness isn't striving, it's *stopping* striving. Be happy with your lot. But that never cut it with her. So I was like, fine, you want more? Okay, let's find you more. Part of it was her job. After Kyle was born she had her mat leave and went back to work and decided she didn't want to be a community care nurse anymore, she wanted something different, more creative maybe, so she started networking and lucked out through an old high school friend and parlayed her health experience into a job with the government, a good paycheque, in PR with the ministry of social services, but that didn't satisfy her either. You know how PR is—it's spin. Not out-and-out lies exactly, but it's not the truth. Some neglected kid hangs himself in a halfway house and she's pumping out deflective press releases about how this government is doing more for kids in halfway houses than any other government ever, and she's like, I don't feel good about this. This is too close to bullshitting. I'd rather do something positive, with a concrete result, like be an interior designer and help people furnish their sunroom, right? The goal there is to make things more pretty, so it's all colour swatches and positivity, right? Like getting to play dress-up for a living. So she quit the government and set out on her own as an interior designer, which I thought was great, but initially, after a couple of friends had her redo their places, it was lean times.

"Then Michael came along. Michael showed up just at the right time, being rich—money-is-no-object kind of rich—and having a big house to redo and reno, top to bottom. He was her lifeline, so she was thrilled, and spent tons of time over there, just with him, and I always suspected he had ulterior motives, because he seemed like a guy with a high sex drive, a voracious lust for life party-hardy guy with a big power boat parked at the yacht club, single again after his *second* divorce, that kind of guy, and here's this good-looking woman coming over and wandering around his house on an almost daily basis. Sylvie's good-looking, there is no doubt. And then I started to get suspicious one time after I overheard them talking on the phone and it sounded super-flirtatious to my ears. Then she went out one day and forgot her phone, and I started scrolling through her texts. Shouldn't do that, I know."

"Curiosity is natural," Rolanda said.

"Yeah. It killed the cat."

"It may have hurt, but it didn't kill you. You're still here."

"Right."

"I admire you for sharing."

My nostrils flared wide. Then I let go. It was like, I'll let the floodgates open. I started to cry.

It felt weird. Just sobbing away without restraint in a little room with a near-stranger. Without turning her eyes or head or even her torso, Rolanda stretched an arm back and retrieved a Kleenex from a box on the shelf behind her, and dangled it before me. At least she didn't drop it like Bugs Bunny. I took it and dabbed. I pulled myself together.

"I shouldn't have looked at her phone, but I had suspicions, right? And I knew her password. So. They were having long conversations, the kind where it's business at the start and then you just keep going, with all kinds of tangential shit taking you hither and yon. I saw where she wrote, 'Nice guys finish last.' And he wrote back, 'Sometimes it's good when the guy finishes last—like in the bedroom.' And then she showered him with frigging emojis—like a thumbs-up, and a blushy face, and a winky face. No pink hearts or anything. But later I snuck another look, and although it was mostly business-related decorating decisions, by then he'd started ending with pink hearts, and flowers. You don't text pink hearts to a married woman, right? I felt like I should say something to Sylvie about that, but in the end I figured, don't say anything, because the project is almost done, and that'll be the end of it. But it wasn't. Next time I looked I saw 'I love you,' and 'I love you too.' That was the killer."

"I can't imagine," Rolanda said.

"Uh huh. Did she leave all this incriminating evidence on her phone, like did she want me to find it? Did she subconsciously want to be found out so she wouldn't have to tell me directly? I knew I had to talk to her, so I got myself primed for the big confrontation, and orchestrated the time and place—kids out of the house at school, me taking a day off work, here we are on a sunny spring morning drinking nice coffee from our cappuccino machine in suburban bliss, except 'There's something I need to ask you about, honey. I've been looking at your phone'—and before I could go any further she started to cry, and told me she loved me and hadn't meant for any of this to happen, but she was also in love with him and was ready to leave me for him. They were planning on telling me soon—they were just waiting for the school year to end so the kids would transition more easily. Worried about the kids, but not about me, obviously."

"That is hard," said Rolanda. "You've been through a lot."

"It gets in your head and it's hard to shed."

She gave me a minute to dab my eyes again, and waited for more, but I was done.

"You know what? I really need to go for a walk. I need to be outside."

When I got home I skipped the house entirely and went around to the back 40 to look for the girls, but Jim next door saw me and waved me over to the fence. That's rare. He usually doesn't have much to do with me. He had a look of gloating on his face.

"Did you hear the news on the deer front?" he asked. "Saanich Council passed a motion last night."

"I missed it."

"The guy from The Pound said they were debating it, remember? Farmers have been so up in arms about deer gnawing crops right down to the rootstalk that Council finally got off their butts and passed a bylaw. Finally, people pestered by deer can do something about it."

"Are you being pestered?"

"You're damn right I am. Klara's scared to leave the house."

"I hope you're not planning on poison or shit like that."

"Not that. Too many housecats and dogs to leave poison laying around. They've settled on something instantly lethal and specifically targeted—they're going to let bow-hunters come in and take deer down."

"Really?"

"Yeah really. Licensed, professional bow-hunters. It's already legal in Langford and Metchosin."

"That is fucking nuts," I said. "Metchosin I can see—a lot of it's wilderness. But if you start flinging arrows around here you'll put out a paperboy's eye."

"These people are professionals. They won't miss. They set up a blind, on scaffolding, put a bait box under it so they're shooting almost straight down, and any miss just goes into the ground. That's the law. Arrows have to be angled down so they stay on the property. And the advantage of professionals is they know all about how to skin and gut an animal, so the meat won't go to waste. All that protein can be shipped to homeless shelters and soup kitchens downtown."

"Now you're shitting me," I said. "Mike from The Pound told us they clean up hundreds of roadkills a year, remember? They've never done a thing with all that meat, so why would they start now? Plus, there'd be so many regulations around processing meat and testing it and labelling it and all that crap, the thing would never fly."

"That's true," he said. "Fucking government."

"Jim, you work for the government." He's a policy analyst or something in the Ministry of Finance. Which sounds even duller than my job.

"I know," he said. "Doesn't make me hate it any less."

"I don't get you at all. What's with all the hatred? My three girls are sweethearts! They're not ruining crops or pestering anyone. Just going about their business being deer. Live and let live."

"We can't even grow tulips," he said. "And one of those deer bit a kid, in case you've forgotten."

"Defending her baby!" I shouted.

Ever see that famous soccer match, that World Cup final where the Muslim Frenchman who's endured a lifetime of trash talk finally can't take it anymore, so he head-butts the Italian loudmouth who's been baiting him all game? Remember that? Name starts with a Z, I think. I'm not much on soccer, but do recall that in his final moment on the world stage, the guy lowered his head like a battering ram and drove it into the enemy's chest. You know what? Standing there looking at Jim's smug, suburban fifty-something face I felt like doing exactly what that Frenchman did. I felt like there would be amazing satisfaction in taking my rock-hard skull and smashing it forcefully against the boney, pencil-thin slats of neighbour Jim's policy-analysing rib cage. I lowered my head, sucked air through my nostrils, felt blood pulse to my forehead. The epicenter of this pulsing blood was the ring mark I got from head-butting Michael's door. I brought the back of my hand up to my face to wipe away a sudden onset of heavy sweat and made contact with my forehead, hard enough to break the scab. I looked at the back of my hand. It was smeared with blood.

Jim looked at me in horror.

The sight of my own red blood sobered me a bit. Jim would be spared. Today at least. "You're lucky," I said. "You don't know how lucky you are."

"You really need to get a grip, Trevor," he said. He was backing away, like he was truly scared of me. I felt a rush, like I had power over him. I was making Jim shit his pants, and I liked it.

PART II

harlene is dead. That is the hardest thing I will ever write in my life.

Yeah. She is dead. Just like that. Life is so precious—tenuous, short, abrupt. You only realise when it hits you in the face. My dead girl in the street.

I was asleep in the back yard. It was well past midnight, I don't know exactly. Cars passing by on the street in front of the house don't usually wake me anymore, but this one did. The sound of a car at high speed is very different from the sound of a car at normal speed, and my ears have grown attuned to these things, sleeping outside. This car made an ominous sound—the windows weren't rolled down but the music from it—the bass—was shaking the air. The very air was vibrating. My eyes popped open, I saw Darlene nearby pull herself to her front knees in order to get up, and then I heard a horrible thud, a lethal thud, there could be no mistake. Instantaneously the hard frantic squeal of brakes.

I jumped up, running from behind the house to the street. A car was stopped, a flashy bright yellow car with tinted windows, the kind of low-slung expensive car rich teenagers think is cool around here. Four kids were spilling out of it and shouting obscenities, not so much to each other but to the air. Near the car was a body. A deer body. From a distance it looked wrong. Its legs were arranged wrong, jutting at wrong angles. Coming closer the body looked wrong too, concave where it should have been convex, like a half-deflated soccer ball kicked in. Then I got up close and could see she was still alive, still trying to hold her head high, nostrils flailing for breath, a vomit of blood pouring from her mouth. I knelt down at her side. Was it Charlene? I knew it was Charlene. She dropped her head to the asphalt in a gesture of surrender, of hopelessness, and in the orange streetlight she fixed her eye on me. I told her, "It's okay, sweetie." I kept saying, "It's going to be okay." Why did I say that when we both knew it wasn't?

The kids from the car came near. There were two girls and two boys. Teenagers. "Is it dead?" asked one of the girls.

"No, she's not."

"It looks messed up," said a boy.

"No way I could stop," said the other. "It just came out of fucking nowhere."

"It flipped right up over the hood, bounced off the windshield, right over top of the roof," said the first boy. "Lucky the windshield didn't smash."

"The airbags didn't go off," said a girl.

"It was a glancing blow," said a boy.

"My head got whacked against the back of your seat," said a girl. "Good thing it's padded."

"We're all alive," said a boy.

"Not the deer," said a boy. "Not for long."

"What should we do?" asked a girl.

"Get the fuck out of here," said a boy.

"We can't leave the scene of an accident," said a girl.

"That's *human* accidents," said a boy. "This is roadkill. You don't have to stick around for roadkill. Plus they might make me take a breathalyser."

"What about the dent in your grill? How will you report it to ICBC?"

"I'll tell them I hit a deer but it didn't die, it ran off into the woods. Because the denting isn't actually that bad."

The whole time they were talking I never took my eyes from Charlene. "Would you kids go? Just go," I said to them. I wanted so very much to be alone with her in her last moments. I cradled my poor dying doe by her neck and held her close.

"Is it, like, your pet or something?" asked a girl.

"Is it dead?" asked a boy. "I think it might be dead now."

"Get the fuck out of here before I smash your skulls in!" I growled. Then I whispered, "Sorry, Charlene."

One of the boys said, "Jesus Christ, buddy, don't overdramatize. We feel shitty enough."

"Let's go," said a girl.

"Wait, I wanna get a picture with my phone," said a boy.

"You take your phone out and I will break every tooth in your head with it," I said.

"Let's go," said a girl again. They got in the car and that absurd earth-shaking bass started up again, just for a second before they killed it. They drove away. Now I was alone with Charlene. Now I could say what I needed to.

"I'm going to find Primula and take care of her, sweetie. You don't have to worry about that. Everything's going to be okay. I'm gonna find her and feed her and I won't ever let her go hungry. I won't ever let anybody hurt her, you can count on that. I'll look out for her, make sure she's raised the right and proper way—"

I was talking to myself. Charlene was dead.

I got a wheelbarrow from behind my garage and rolled it up to the street. On my knees on the street I scraped my knuckles trying to slide my hands under her body. She was still flexible, no rigor mortis. Flexible but heavy as hell. On my knees I lifted her and poured her into the wheelbarrow, which tipped over and dumped her back onto the street. It was just too ridiculous. I was crying. Walking on my knees on the road like a penitent, putting the wheelbarrow back level, doing it all over again. My back is shot now, but I got her in. No way I was going to let Saanich Pound chuck her in the back of a truck and dump her wherever the hell they've dumped a thousand other corpses. In the wheelbarrow, her head and neck looked all scrunched up and uncomfortable, and her legs were splayed upward like the drones of a bagpipe. It was hard to see her like that, looking so undignified.

When I got her to the back yard I tipped her out carefully as I could, laid her out on the grass and tried to arrange her in a pose that looked natural, like she was at rest. Under her belly there were dribbles of milk leaking from her teats. Milk meant for Primula. I was thinking crazy thoughts, like maybe I should try to squeeze the milk out and collect it in a bottle and save it for Primula, for her to drink later. My mind was filled with possible complications or consequences coming from me presenting a little fawn with her dead mother's milk. Would she take it? Would she know her mom was dead? Would she think I did it?

I squeezed at her teats experimentally, but it felt like nothing good would come from trying harder. I had no technique and she was dead. I got the shovel and dug a hole, not really deep enough, because eighteen inches down I hit clay. Digging with a shovel felt good, a way of working the grief out. By morning light, around 5 a.m., I put her in the hole and filled it in. I topped it with clods of grass with their roots intact that I'd set aside, and it was a pretty good job, I thought. Not level, obviously. A burial mound. But the grass would live, regrow, reconnect into the earth, and feed off of Charlene. The circle of life. I took the garden hose and watered the mound, watched the water run off it and soak into the ground. Then I rinsed the blood off the wheelbarrow, some of it her blood and some of it mine from my scraped knuckles.

I tried to think of an appropriate ceremony. Last rites. A speech? Deer don't have use for words. Tears came. I wanted to give her some part of me. I wet my fingers with my tears and knelt and wiped them on the clods of grass. I hacked up some phlegm from my throat and spat it on the grave, giving some part of me as an offering to mingle in the earth with her. I should have spread my tears directly onto her coat before I buried her, I should have anointed her body before I'd covered her over with earth. I had an urge to pee on the mound of earth, to offer something pungent and robust. Does that make sense? It would to a deer.

I felt justified in doing it. I unzipped and took out my penis and tried to relax and let it flow but then a whiff came to me from the thicket, deep, pungent, distracting. What was it? A feminine scent for sure. Human? Deer? Parts of both maybe—woman and doe, bound together. Was I hallucinating? Can you hallucinate a smell? A movement in the branches, a rustle of leaves, and a sense of being watched made me self-conscious, made me tuck my cock back in. Scanning the foliage in the gathering light of morning I thought I saw a face, a human face, or was it a deer face? Something in between? Just for a sec it could be clearly seen through a gap in the branches, and just for a sec, our eyes met, like she wanted me to know she existed, but nothing more. She was there and gone.

Did it really happen?

nd where was Primula? I had to find Primula. It was light enough now to look for her. I went back into the thicket, scanning the underbrush all the way through to that broken-down fence that was the boundary of Mount Doug. No sign of her. If she was hunkered down hiding, with her camouflage I'd pretty much need to step on her to find her. I tried to peek into the tangle of blackberries. I called her name, which set some dogs barking in the distance.

I gave up and headed back toward the house, and there was Darlene, sniffing at Charlene's burial mound, and guess who was with her?

Yes, Primula was dancing and gamboling around her, or so I thought at first glance, but then I realised she was trying to get at Darlene's teats. She looked downright desperate to get her lips onto Darlene's tits. Darlene, not having any milk or maternal instinct, didn't like that—she twisted and hit my hungry little fawn with a sharp kick that connected with a thud against Primula's chest and sent her airborne. She crash-landed on the grass and then leapt back to her feet all in one motion like a miniature gymnast. Thinking about the damage razor-sharp hooves can do, I was worried she might be cut. I could see no blood, but she had definitely learned her lesson. No way was she going to try that again.

She gave a plaintive little bleat, and looked at me like, *Now what do I do?*

"I'll get you some milk," I said.

I went inside and googled baby fawn food. Who knew it was a fucking industry? First thing I saw told me tractor supply stores carry wildlife replacement milk—there's an amazing smorgasbord of formulas for sale. Squirrels, raccoons, possums, cottontails, white-tailed deer, black-tailed deer, beavers (the last one also recommended for bears, otters and sea lions) all have their own formulas. All very curious and amusing under normal circumstances, but I was worried and in a hurry. A google of tractor supply stores showed the closest to be in Duncan, a long drive over the Malahat. Clicking some more taught me goat milk also works for fawns, the same goat milk that new-age types drink. Goat milk is easy in Gordon Head.

So I ran over to Rootcellar to get goat milk, forgetting how early in the morning it was. The place was closed. *Fuck! I need that fucking goat milk!* Then I remembered Thrifty's at Tuscany Village is open 24 hours. I went there, they had goat milk. Yay! Along with it I bought some baby bottles, nipples and all. The cashier was a young guy with an overly-fussy precise haircut, almost shaved on the sides but with just enough left on top to pull back and tie in a teensy pony-tail. It felt like he was communicating something with his hair. I kept staring at it, hoping to figure out what. "Whatcha feeding?" he asked.

"Pardon me?"

"You're buying goat's milk and baby bottles—that can't be for a kid. A human kid, I mean."

"Oh. Right. It's for a fawn."

"I was gonna say that. My mom tried that one time when I was little. We rescued a fawn. It didn't go too well."

"What happened?"

"It got weaker and weaker and eventually lay down by the back door and wouldn't get up. Me and my mom made a little bed for it with a blanket. My mom's boyfriend refused to let it in the house. Then we called ARC; they came and took it. My mom was all like, 'Oh, Fawnie is being so well-looked-after now that soon they'll let him go free in the forest to live with all his deer friends.' She didn't want to shatter my childhood illusions. Fawnie died though. She told me years later when she thought I could handle it."

"ARC—what's that?"

"Animal Rescue...something that starts with C."

I wondered for just a sec whether I should phone ARC. No! Fawnie died there. Primula was not going to die under my watch.

Back home I warmed some goat milk in a bottle in the microwave, tested it on my wrist just like I used to do once upon a time with my own ingrate kinder, and took it out back. No sign of Darlene or Marlene—or Primula. I went back to the edge of the thicket, calling her name softly, and lo and behold she did come, considering me through the leaves with those big soft eyes from a safe distance. I knelt down and shook the bottle gently, made soothing cooing sounds, and she came forward, all nerves, ready to take off at the first sudden movement. "Come here, silly," I kept saying, and she inched closer and closer until she was practically on my lap. I held the bottle upside down, at about the height of her mother's teats, and she touched it with her tongue tentatively, then backed off at the unfamiliar taste. But hunger won out and she came back committed. She started slurping away, but she was working too hard—the hole in the nipple was too small for her to get a good draw of liquid. I told myself to take scissors and nick the tip of the nipple next time to make the hole bigger.

It made me feel happy to be certain there would be a next time.

She finished the bottle and looked at me: *Is that all?* "I'll get you another one," I said. Inside I did a refill and slit the nipple a bit, and brought it back out. She did a little happy dance at the sight of me, a butterfly's flutter. This time she drank only half before she was full, blinking and swaying drowsily on her feet. "Nap time," I whispered, and I led her over to the grassy shade under a Garry Oak, where I sat down and coaxed her to sit beside me. She did. In fact she placed her head on my lap, and I felt absolutely blissful, like some kind of human–non-human telepathical connection was being attained. All the plants around me were my partners and equals and I stopped thinking in words and heard them speak. Not speak, exactly, because there were no words, but they were asserting their aliveness. Then the spell was broken because Primula got up and started to poop.

Remember Kyle calling fawn poop cottage cheese? That's pretty much what it looked like. It was white and runny and was plopping out of her butt onto the ground. She hadn't turned away from me to do her business modestly; in fact, she was pretty much doing it in my face, telling me it was my problem to deal with. The mom at this early age eats the cheesy poop as it emerges, and licks the butt clean, to protect the wee one from taking on tell-tale smells that attract predators, remember? Predators. I thought of the pit-bulls that live two streets over. What if they broke out? It's happened before. It was incumbent upon me to keep them from smelling Primula! I had to keep things tidy. She finished her business and did a stretch of her back legs, and then circled around a couple of times, ending with her butt right in my face again. *Clean me up!* That's what she wanted. Her little black tail was still sticking straight up, lifted like the lid of a toilet seat. I got a Kleenex out of my pocket and dabbed at her bum hole with it. It wasn't gross or anything, not like the stench of human shit.

She flinched a little, but accepted my dabbing even if it wasn't as soft, wet and massaging as the mother's tongue she was used to. "Sorry sweetie, this is as good as you get from me," I said. The Kleenex got soaked after half the job and I tossed it, and noticed I got a cottage-cheesy-looking bit on my pinky. Human nature is animal nature—you have to smell new smells, it can't be helped. I gave it a good sniff. It smelled okay. Cheesy. Nothing offensive. Taste? I stuck the tip of my tongue out and made contact, just the lightest of touches. It was tasteless. Not totally, but less flavourful than expected. No urge to do it twice. I thought of Charlene doing it tenderly, with a mother's love, and I choked up, fighting tears. Poor Charlene.

I went in the house and got a warm wet washcloth to do the job right, but when I came back out, Primula had changed her demeanor and wouldn't let me near her butt. I wiped at the wee pile of cheesy whiteness she'd made on the grass and dropped the washcloth in the garbage bin in the carport. Then I went out back to my sleeping bag under the tarp because suddenly I was dead tired. Primula was restless, and I kept telling her Charlene was fine and would be back soon—I didn't like lying but what could I say? Eventually she curled up nearby in the shade, close to me, but not too close.

The phone rang in the house. Landline. These days I keep it near an open window. It woke me up and sent Primula racing in terror to the thicket. The phone is set to ring ten times before it clicks over to the machine. I went inside and picked up on the seventh. It was Mona.

"Where are you Trevor?"

"I'm at home."

"I know that. What I mean is, why aren't you at work?"

"Oh fuck," I said. "I forgot about that."

"You forgot?"

"I had an emergency. A family matter."

"Oh no. I'm sorry. What's going on?"

"Charlene died. In the night. I buried her and now I'm looking after Primula."

The line was quiet for a minute. "Are you talking about deer here?"

"Yes."

"And that's a family matter?"

"Yes."

"Technically, I'm not sure about that, Trevor. I don't recall the collective agreement making any mention of pets as a reason to miss work."

"She wasn't a pet. I'm not shirking work, I just forgot. A lot happened. Do you hear what I'm telling you? Charlene died in my fucking arms! And now there's a little girl named Primula all alone in the world."

"I am sorry. Should you call some Animal Rescue people? The ARC?"

"This is her home," I said. "She's better off here. I'm taking care of her."

"I'm glad you care about her. But there are other things you need to take care of too, Trevor. You're only fifteen minutes late right now. If you get here before 9:30 that's only half an hour. I'll forgive you that, because of your emergency."

"I'm coming in. I'm on my way."

Primula was in the thicket somewhere. I yelled, "I'll be back, sweetie! Just hang in there." Then I drove straight to the Care Home, went straight downstairs to my desk in the bunker, fired up the computer, looked at all my unanswered emails, and started to cry.

Was it for Charlene? Partly. But also for myself. Sad desk, windowless room, office hours—how could that express who I am and who I want to be?

Mona came with a box of Kleenex. I took three. "You look a sight, Trevor," she said. "Did you sleep in those clothes?"

"You told me to get here ASAP."

"If I'd known what you looked like, I would have told you to get changed first. Is that—is that dried blood on your shirt?"

"That's Charlene's blood."

"*Trevor.*"

"I was holding her in my arms, in the street."

"You can't come to work in a bloody shirt. Stand up for me."

As I stood I could smell my armpits. There was no doubt I stank really bad. My chest itched like crazy and I scratched it under my shirt. The hairs there seemed thicker than what I'm used to.

"Your pants are even worse," she said. "Do you have a change of clothes in your locker?"

"No."

"What am I going to do with you?"

"Send me home."

"I wish I could but Georgina's away and Melody is—"

"I'm going now."

"I can cover for you for an hour. Can you please go home and have a shower, clean yourself up?"

"That's the scent of death."

"What?"

"The scent of death. That's what it smells like."

"Don't scare me, Trevor. You need to listen to me—"

I stopped listening. Words were bars of a cage. Break out. Get away. Soon almost running. It felt good to live by instinct. Stop talking and go where I need to be. I sprinted across the parking lot, zig-zagging between cars, got back in my car and made a beeline for home. Home to take care of my baby.

I couldn't find her at first. Gave up. Tried to relax. Took a long hot shower. It didn't feel as good as I hoped it would. Running the soap across my torso and legs felt peculiar—rubbing down was fine, but up was like working against stubble.

I went on the internet to figure out how often I should feed goat milk to a fawn. Every fucking thing is on the internet, which still amazes me because I am forty-nine years old and remember the Dark Ages when if you wanted to know how to do some new thing that you had no clue how to do, you either just had at 'er with gusto and guesswork, or you talked to someone who knew how to do it, or you put on your coat and went down to the public library and got a book about it. And often at the library they didn't even have the book or someone else had it signed out and it wouldn't be back for weeks. Now all it takes is a single phrase and a single click and I was led to a very dense, thorough website put up by the North American Deer Farmers Association, which said I should feed her 10 to 20 percent of her body weight every day. How much did she weigh? Apparently fawns weigh about six pounds when born. She was now maybe a week old. I figured the best thing would be to take my bathroom scale, weigh myself, go find her, pick her up in my arms and stand on the scale, do a simple subtraction, then I'd know for sure what she weighs. Online I ordered something called "First Fawn," which is a food supplement that makes fawns super healthy and contains colostrum, which is essential. Lots of things are essential—they were telling me I needed to give antibiotic shots but I figured let's keep her wild as we can and not go there. I hate getting needles myself and have never tried to give someone else one. She would squirm and probably I'd poke her eye out and she'd hate me forever.

I took the bathroom scale outside and looked for her in the thicket, figuring she wouldn't stray far. After twenty minutes of mounting anxiety I came up empty. It was making me angry. *Come out, little ingrate!* Then I saw her in Jim and Klara's back yard, kind of half sitting, half laying down, content as anything, sleepy-headed in the sun.

"Primula!"

Her ears twitched and swiveled, and she lifted her head to look at me.

"Stay right there, I'll be right over."

Through the gate I entered into their private domain of shorn monocultural grass. Darlene let me get close to her, but before I could pick her up she sprang to her feet and darted to the three-foot fence and all in a single beautiful fluid motion she jumped over it, nearly scaling it cleanly, but she clipped her back hooves against the top bar and tumbled over to land with a clumsy thud in my long grass. She got to her feet, apparently none the worse for wear, and looked at me coldly.

"Be careful," I said.

"You're wasting your breath. She doesn't speak English."

I turned around and there was Jim, right behind me.

"I know that. It's about the tone," I said. "She picks up on the tone, and knows I'm on her side."

"What's with the bathroom scale?"

I explained.

"Jesus Christ man, just take a hammer to her skull, save yourself a load of trouble."

"Don't say that. She has a right to live, same as we do."

"No she doesn't. She has no legal protections anymore, now Saanich has passed that new bylaw. I've already found someone who'll take care of her."

"You what?"

"I found a bow-hunter. Believe it or not it's a woman. I was a bit surprised at first, but I'm good with that—a woman is more likely to be careful with her shot, and kill more humanely, don't you think?"

I opened my mouth to speak but something ignited in my head like a burning fury. It felt at my temples like two flaming meteorites had crashed with sudden impact against my skull, then stuck there, embedded deep and hard like branding irons. I saw red, then grey. The world was black and white, with no colour. I breathed through my nose. Big snorts. Humungous snorts.

Jim looked frightened. His eyes went wide. He took a step back and I took three forward, and my chest almost bumped his chest. It might even have touched it.

He backed away some more. "Watch what you're doing, Trevor, you're on private property." These weren't the words of a brave man asserting his rights, but a diminished man. An insignificant man.

"I'm going to kick your ass now," I said.

"No you're not."

"Oh yes I am!" I lowered my head and charged, loaded up with single-minded intent to maim and mangle, but because my head was lowered my aim was poor, and the sweet glorious thud of impact never came. He'd scrambled aside. I lifted my head. "There you are, you shifty bastard!"

"What the fuck? Are you nuts, man?" His voice had gone all high-pitched and preadolescent. He turned and hightailed it toward his house, and I ran after him, tracking him like a predator right up to his back door. He slipped inside and I felt high as a kite. I'd won! I felt like the guys that hoist the Stanley Cup while the PA blasts "We Are The Champions"! I'd entered some glorious newfound consciousness, where power is pure strength, and action is everything. To put an exclamation point on it I butted my forehead against the glass of his back door like a matador thrusting home the final blade.

Second time I've hit a door with my head lately, I know. First time was out of frustration and powerlessness, but this time it felt so good! It's weird but feels so good. His door was the outer of two doors, a big glass pane I could have butted hard and broken. But no, that was not my intent. This head butt was firm, but not glass-shattering. It was a symbol of my victory over Jim. A symbol that I was powerful, yet could show restraint. I could see him cowering behind the glass before he closed the windowless inner door, and then I was alone. The glass where my forehead had just struck it was smudged red. I must have ripped Sylvie's peephole scab again. No mind. I liked it that way. A dab of blood, a mark he'd need to clean off, and when he wiped at it with paper towel and Windex, he would tremble at my fearlessness.

Then it was feeding time. It went well. Primula trusts me. She let me stroke her soft coat while she sucked at the bottle—the only time all day I felt calm and relaxed. I promised myself I'd stop fussing about how much she eats. Offer it up six times a day and let her go at it until she's full. Googling told me that was right. She'd had nearly a week's worth of her mom's milk, so that should have given her a good start, a crucial dose of colostrum. The goat milk must contain some too. That's all I can do.

I went over to Rootcellar to get more milk, which I didn't want to but I had to. It makes me ill at ease whenever we're apart—Rootcellar is only a couple of kilometres, but still, driving away like that puts me out of rescue range. I tell myself she's fine, and no harm will come to her while I'm gone, but still I worry. She's old enough to wander off on her own, too young to understand the dangers of streets and cars, and pit bulls unchained in back yards. I really wish I could just put her in the house. She'd be safe in the house. But she wouldn't be wild.

Rootcellar has a good deal on goat milk right now, in two-litre jugs. That should have relaxed me, helped me calm down, knowing a plentiful supply is always close at hand, but instead I kept charging around the place in panicky beat-the-clock mode, rushing past pyramids of oranges and red peppers and actually breaking out in a cold sweat. Indoor shopping I don't like. Indoor anything I don't like. I like outdoors. Carry on, Trevor—I actually had to tell myself that. Fight the claustrophobia. The agoraphobia. All the other phobias.

Usually at Rootcellar I go to the deli counter and get some mild Hungarian salami for lunchtime sandwiches, but more and more lately the thought of meat turns my stomach, so today I said, "I feel like some vegetarian salami, do you have that?" and the girl behind the glass case said they had something called "veggie salami parmesano," which is a veggie salami coated in parmesan cheese. When they slice it, the Parmesan stays in a circle of cheesy fattiness around the slice like the fiery ring of a solar eclipse. It looked good. "Is it good?" She picked up a single slice with her tongs and held it out to me. I folded it in half, then a quarter, and popped it in my mouth, kind of hurriedly and distractedly, like I do most things lately. I chomped down hard and my teeth sank into the side of my mouth. *"Yeaowww!!!"*

Excruciating hurt. Behind the counter the girl was staring into my face expectantly, waiting for the verdict. She was expecting me to say something like, "Hey, this salami par-mesano is really scrumptious." Instead she saw tears clog my eyes.

I hung my head to avoid eye contact. My mind was messed up by severe pain at that moment but what I did next was peculiar and I'm troubled even now thinking about it. I wanted to flee, that was the base urge, just to get the hell out of there, and I meant to just walk away, not caring if she thought I was strange. Instead of coolly swivelling on my heel and sauntering on my merry way, which is what in my mind I knew I should aim for, my body took over and made the decision on some physical level. I actually *bounded* away. My legs were suddenly like super springs, the perfect tools to get me gone.

So there I was leaping across the store, and I turned a corner down an aisle where a pile of pre-cooked hams sat in a cooler, feeling a bit safer once I was out of sight of that deli girl. I brought my hand to my face and cupped my jaw tenderly, and slowly, delicately, chewed the salami until it was like cud, like a wad of gum in its size and shape, and then I spat it onto my hand and dropped it behind a ham. I can't tell you whether it was good or not, I just wanted it out of my mouth. I wiped the tears from my eyes and composed myself. I knew the deli girl wouldn't follow me, but for some reason I had to be certain. I tiptoed back to the corner and peeked past the hams, just far enough to see her behind the counter. She was definitely over me, already onto the next customer. *What a relief.* Why such a relief? I can't say.

In the car driving home, I felt inside my mouth with my fingers. My molars had torn my flesh. My teeth felt bigger. No denying it. My teeth *are* bigger.

Mona has put me on stress leave for a week.

Stress leave? Really?

When the ladies in my office pull stress leave, I'm super dismissive. I mean, really—we live in the safest, most laid-back corner of the entire planet, Victoria fucking British Columbia Canada, for fuck's sakes, where the air is clean, the water's pure, the streets are swept, where every year Conde Nast ranks it top ten for travellers and the UN ranks it top three for livability, and here in our little office we've got secure jobs and pension plans, and these women need stress leave? Don't they watch the news? Don't they see what's going on in Syria or Sudan or some other nightmare of a bombed-out sun-fried sandstorm wasteland? People losing their homes, their livelihoods, their loved ones—that's fucking stress, okay?

That's exactly what I said to Rolanda today. I was venting, it felt good, I was getting worked up, but maybe I crossed a line. I denigrated middle-class Canadian stress, forgetting that Rolanda's life and livelihood is devoted to relieving it. Not nice. I started pacing her little room, feeling totally penned in. Any enclosed space feels like prison these days, but that one's especially bad. She's decorated it to make it some feminine ideal of cozy, but cozy doesn't cut it, I need long sight lines and escape routes or else I get twitchy, I pace like a Rottweiler in a dog run. Back and forth, back and forth.

She said to me, "Please sit down Trevor," and I said I couldn't.

She said, "You're actually making me nervous, sit down and let's do a meditation together."

I said, "I can't sit, I feel like, Pan."

It was the first time I'd ever said that, or even thought it, but it was true. You know how Pan is half man, half goat? A man's head, arms and torso, and a goat's butt and legs? That's how I feel these days. I feel like my legs are not human legs. They ache when I sit. They need motion.

"If you can't sit, then you can lie down if you want," she said.

That actually sounded good. They don't ache when I lie down.

I slumped to the floor and twisted my rump so I could spread my legs like half a swastika, and it settled me. Sort of. I was still worked up and claustrophobic. I was breathing hard through my nose. Snorting. In a calm, soothing voice Rolanda told me she wanted me to relax, clear my mind, and not feel I have to live up to anything or anyone. I was nodding in agreement, feeling very tired but comfortable, my legs splayed on the floor and my head resting on the velvety padded seat of an armchair. Then the very next thing I remember is her calling my name softly, waking me up ever so gently. She whispered, "I thought I would let you sleep;

you seemed to want it so very badly. Letting you have a little nap might be a way to improve your associations with the space we're in."

I was grateful to her for that. I did feel better, although I had a hard time getting my legs under me to get up. I put my elbows on the chair and my legs tried to go from kneeling to standing with my elbows still dug into the chair, so I was all bent forward funny, then pushing up one arm at a time to get erect. Getting *homo erectus* was never so much work. I was doing it like how Darlene and Marlene do it. And Charlene of course. Poor Charlene.

First thing I did after I got home—okay, second thing, the first was I had to find Primula and feed her goat milk, singing "A Spoon Full of Sugar Helps the Medicine Go Down" to her, telling her her name was now Primula Poppins—was go to the computer and look up Pan, which got me six million hits and pix of satyrs, which to the Greeks were half-horses and to the Romans were half-goats. Horse or goat, horny drunkards, the lot of them. I got more specific and googled "half man half deer" and then refined it to "half man half stag," because stags have antlers and if you want to know, I wish I had antlers. Then when I bash my head against things, like I've been wanting to do a lot lately, I could do some serious damage. So I clicked the "images for" link and my brain just about exploded out of my head! Pinterest paintings popped up by the hundreds of a fantastical creature that was half-stag, half-man. Some of them were well-rendered and realistic, some were cartoonish and cheesy, but collectively they spoke to me. They did more than speak—they shook me by the shoulders and screamed in my face! I felt like crying. This beautiful brooding image of a half-man half-stag lurking in the misty woods was me! That's how I feel! That's who I want to be!

PART III

Well that was too fucking sudden.

Guess what I saw in Jim and Klara's back yard?

Ten feet of metal scaffolding, and on top of it, a hunter's blind.

Yes. A hunter's blind.

I cannot believe this. It's elaborate and ridiculous, all burlap and camouflage, meant for the deep woods, perched one storey up on heavy-duty construction scaffolding, smack dab in the middle of their perfect pool-table of a back lawn, right next to their pseudo-wicker plastic patio furniture from Walmart.

This cannot stand. That's what I thought when I looked at it. *This has to come down. Fuck private property, I'm going to march on over and deal with it.* So I did. Not marched— bounded, like in Rootcellar. My legs have a lot of spring in them these days, especially when I'm riled. And I was riled.

"Anybody in there?"

No answer. I felt like maybe it was a Trojan Horse, that there might be someone up there who didn't want me to know they were in there. I mean, that's the whole purpose of a hunting blind, right? From a distance it looked sturdy and boxlike, but close up you could see it was basically a tent, just some hollow metal tubes with some camouflage fabric draped over. On each side, it had a slit of gauzier material you could peek out through like the little rectangle of mesh women who wear burkas look out through, and at the back you could see a slit in the fabric you could lift and enter. I climbed up towards it and the whole thing shook like an earthquake. It was really not very stable at all. The feet of the scaffolding had not been nailed down to the lawn with spikes or pegs. Instead they rested on four pieces of plywood, each the size of a welcome mat. With each rung I climbed, my weight was enough to lift the two legs opposite off the plywood for a sec. Gave me a queasy feeling. I got up high enough to pull back the fabric and peek inside. There was nothing but one of Jim and Klara's pseudo-wicker patio chairs sitting on bare planks. On the chair was a book. A brick-thick romance novel. Nora Roberts. Sylvie used to like those.

Coming down the ladder I noticed a pile of dried peas laid out on the lawn, just as if someone had tipped and emptied a five-pound sack. A bait station, meant to lure deer. The angle down to it from the blind was steep enough that any arrow that missed would thwack harmlessly into the grass. That's what the bylaw demands. I went over and stirred the peas with the toe of my shoe, just looking them over. Just a day or two ago I read somewhere (when I was figuring out what to feed Primula) that peas are the best thing to feed deer, because corn is bad for them, and oats and other grains will get gobbled up by birds, squirrels, raccoons, and rats.

Klara came out her back door. I noticed they haven't cleaned the blood off the glass where I bashed it with my forehead the other day. It's changed colour to a deep brown smudge with one dried rivulet running down like the drip from a bad paint job.

"Don't touch the peas, Trevor," she said. She came down the two steps onto her patio, as if to prove she wasn't scared to come near me. But I could tell she was scared to come near me. We talked from twenty feet apart.

"I can't believe you guys are serious," I said.

"Jim is. It's Jim, more than me."

"And Jim always gets his way?"

"No. In fact Jim seldom gets his way," she said, trying to smile. "And the secret to that is to let him get his way sometimes, when he really cares about something. He sees it as us versus them, and he just can't let the deer win."

"Yeah, heaven forbid that the deer who were here first should be the ones to win."

"They were here first, but there were natural mechanisms in place to keep their numbers down," she said. "Cougars and wolves would have been here too. But we can't have cougars and wolves running around, so we need to step in and do the job for them. This is legal now. Obviously a lot of people think it's a good idea."

"I don't."

"We do. We've got the proper permits, and we've hired someone who takes a holistic approach—she takes the carcass away and has it butchered, so that the meat gets used, and nothing goes to waste. You might be very impressed with her."

"I doubt it."

"Trevor, why are you on our property?"

I could feel my nostrils flare wide. "I'm beginning to really hate that word, 'property.'"

"Property is what makes us safe," said Klara.

"What do you mean?"

"Well, knowing this is my property and you can't come over here without permission makes me feel like there's a buffer zone. A safe space."

"And yet here I am, without permission."

"Yes. And I'm going to have to ask you to leave."

"You don't feel safe?"

"The best answer to that question is to look at my door."

"I saw that. You still haven't cleaned it up."

"No. Jim said to leave it, just in case there are more incidents."

"What, you'll show it to the police or something?"

She took a minute to chose her words carefully. "It's proof that something happened."

We had a stare down.

"Okay," I said. "I get it. Everybody needs their space. I violated yours, so I'm going to get off it now. But let me tell you something. Darlene, Marlene and Primula may be nothing more than pests to you, but to me they're loved ones. And if any of them are harmed, there will be retribution. You understand me? Retribution."

"I'll make a note of that," she said. "For the police."

The land line in the house pretty much sits there mute, like a relic. The only person that calls it is Mona. But it rang and it wasn't Mona, it was my friend Randall. We go way back, back to high school; we bonded smoking weed on summer weekends at Willows Beach, ogling the Oak Bay girls who turned up their pert little noses at us. We were Saanich geeks—an inferior species, according to those perfectly tanned daughters of wealth and splendour. We're still geeks, but now we're pushing fifty and we hardly ever see each other, Randall and me. So it was a bit odd, how insistent and super-keen Randall sounded about wanting to see me. He was like, "Anytime's good. Tonight? Tomorrow night? If you're up for it, even right now works."

"What happened? Something happen? You and Margo split or something?" Margo's his wife. They were at each other's throats for years but lately seem to have settled into resigned indifference, or benign neglect. Stopped fighting in front of company, anyhow.

"What? No, nothing like that. I just want to see you, bud."

"Ah, gee, I don't know, I got things to do."

"Like what?"

"I don't know. I just do." I didn't want to get into it about Charlene dying and leaving Primula for me to look after, and how that's my primary focus now. I knew he'd treat it like a joke. Banter has always been the keystone of how we relate.

"Are you working tomorrow?"

"No."

"Then tonight is perfect, my man! Margo's got her book club so I'm free as a bird. You and me'll have an anti-book club, we'll hit Spinnakers and drink a bunch of beer and shoot the shit like old times. It's warm enough to sit on the patio. Come on, bud. Don't leave me hanging."

He wouldn't let it go, so I caved. What the hell, it might even be good for me.

Two hours later we were sitting across from each other at Spinnakers looking out at the choppy waters of the Inner Harbour. A cool North Pacific breeze had picked up, so we were upstairs, inside, looking at the view through windows. The beer came and it was good, but the smell was overpowering. I've never been the kind of beer snob who says things like This beer is quite hoppy, but now it felt like I could even break down the smell into constituent parts. Hops, barley, malt, even the water seemed to have minerals in it, like it came from a unique spring. But what the hell, it smelled great, tasted good and hit me fast, loosened me up more than I've felt in a long time. *Yes! This is what I need more of—human companionship!* The emergency exit door was propped open and added to the calming view of the harbour beyond. Good beer, trusted company, an escape route with long sight lines—it was almost perfect. The single unsettling aspect was a big fucking elk head mounted on the wall. The way we were sitting I had to turn ninety degrees to see it, so it wasn't too bad, but when I did glance over there, it felt like Big Old Elk was staring me down, giving me the evil eye, and it triggered emotions. In words, those emotions could be summarized as, *What are you looking at, Motherfucker????* *YOU WANNA START SOMETHING????* You can't stop an emotion, only rationalize it. Remember I told you how deer sit to avoid direct eye contact with each other? I totally get that.

What do you talk about with an old friend? Well I hadn't seen the guy for many moons, so he wanted to get caught up on what felt like barely relevant ancient history to me—the divorce, and who got what. I got the house, my beloved

Gordon's Head, and Randall said I scored big time. "Are you taking good care of it?" he asked.

"What do you mean?"

"Are you looking after it? Maintaining it—keeping it clean?"

"No, it's a complete sty. What the fuck kind of question is that? What's it to you?"

"I'm just curious. You might want to sell at some point. Don't neglect it."

"I'll keep that in mind, but I'm staying put. I feel anchored there. It's my territory. I've got responsibilities and commitments there—"

I was about to tell him about Primula, but Randall interrupted. "How are you feeling physically?"

"Jeez, I've never seen you so concerned about me."

"I'm your friend. For thirty plus years. It's natural."

"I guess. Thank you. You really want to know how I'm feeling?"

"Of course. Like, for example, how did you get that scab in the middle of your forehead?"

"You like that?"

"Gives you that Cyclops look."

"Not Cyclops. That's one eye. I've got three."

"Right. The third eye. That's all about clairvoyance, right?"

"Yeah. I can read your mind."

"I hope not."

"I can."

"Then what am I thinking?"

"You're thinking I'm fucking nuts."

"Shit! That's pretty good, Trevor. Points for that."

Were we just bantering, or was it true? Doesn't matter. In perfect physical synchronicity we both lifted our pints and drained a good guzzle.

"But seriously," he said.

"Seriously, my friend? I've got all kinds of weird shit going on. I'm growing new teeth in my mouth. Big ones. My jaw wants to jut out all the time."

"I noticed you were biting your lip funny."

"Can't help it. And I've got weird rashes on my chest and back, and my hair is growing thicker and coarser on my legs. I'm even growing some on my butt."

"No shit. What do you think that's about?"

"I don't know." The alcohol made me feel warm and sentimental and receptive to his questions, and I started saying things I have never said out loud before, not even written down in this journal, either. "I've got two points of intense pain, here, hidden in the hair just above my temples. When I close my eyes and rub the spots it feels like something hard and bonelike is growing there. I picture antlers in my mind. I don't just picture antlers, I desire antlers. I have antler envy."

"You're scaring me," Randall said. "That is fucking weird."

"Yeah. You know what else is weird? My cock. It feels like it's growing thicker. Sturdier. More like a root."

"We can all dream."

"I'm serious. It's primordial. Like a root. Like it springs from the earth."

"Well if it's got dirt on it wash it off before you use it."

"It's not a joke."

"I don't know, man. Let's change the subject."

"Yeah. Probably the first time I ever talked about my cock with you. Or matters sexual."

"And hopefully the last."

"Sylvie used to complain about that," I said.

"Your cock?"

"No, not my cock, idiot. The fact that I didn't like to talk about matters sexual. She was always like, 'You never *ask* for anything.' Like, when we were doing it, I would never tell her what I wanted her to do to me, or what I wanted to do to her."

"I'm a talker," Randall said.

"Not me. Not at all. I kind of like to get in a groove, and let bodies do what they need to do. Keep it like a silent ritual. Interrupting it with chatter would just be a distraction."

"Not talking would lead to a kind of sameness, though, right? Same old same old, time after time."

"I guess so."

"You look really bummed out right now."

The alcohol was making me loose-lipped. "I'm thinking about something she said to me one time. This was not long after she left. There's a phase you go through—the demanding-answers phase. The blindsided, how-could-you phase, where it's still super fresh and everything cuts to the bone. I was deep in that phase. 'How? Why?' And she said something like 'He's way more adventurous.'"

"Ouch."

"Yeah—as soon as she said it she looked sorry for me, like she wished she hadn't, and that only made it worse. Like, 'You're a shitty lover—oohh I'm so sorry I said that!'"

"I'm going to grab us a couple more pints," Randall said. While he was over at the bar I drifted off into a bit of a reverie, remembering the domestic bliss of sexual union with Sylvie, which over the course of our marriage evolved into a ritual of doing it once a week on Saturday night. We would close and lock the bedroom door so if the kids woke up and wanted to come to our bed they wouldn't stumble in and catch us all frothy and grunting and exposed. That would have been embarrassing to all concerned, so we would lock the door and make love without that worry, spiralling up together to that tremendous delirium of orgasm—hers first, mine second, naturally, then ten minutes of snuggling and half-snoozing and then, guess what? Time to get up, wipe up, and—time for a bedtime snack! We'd joke about how funny it was: that we could thrash away on sweaty sheets, working ourselves into this feverish, out-of-body, ecstatic, indescribable apex of sensation that is the human orgasm, and then fifteen minutes later, after she'd had a little nap on my chest and I'd shriveled and shrank inside her and plopped out of her, we could get up from our bed and put on baggy PJs and go sit on separate couches in the living room munching cereal from bowls, reading magazines spread open on the padded arms of the couches, each in our separate universe.

The thing about our sex life is, to me it was always good—not frequent maybe, but what the hell, people lie to pollsters and census takers about how often they fuck, that's what I think. No one wants to sound like a loser doing it once a month. Once a week seemed to be our sweet spot—that's what it evolved into without conscious discussion. You can't ever really know what a woman is feeling, and she can't know what a man feels either. But you learn from their reactions what works. I thought it was perfect. I looked forward to Saturday night. I never tired of her body. The best sex is a partnership, right? You're committing yourself to the wholeness of it, happily doing your share and receiving your share in return. Tit for tat. It's like dancing. We always danced well together too, although we haven't done that in years and will likely never dance together again. Actually I suppose we will, at the kids' weddings. That'll be bittersweet and painful. How far off is that? Ten, fifteen, twenty years? In twenty years I'll be like, seventy and decrepit. Michael will watch us condescendingly—he'll be older than me but still look fit and tanned and rich, the bastard, and after my obligatory *pro forma* performance he'll take his rightful place in the centre of the celebration and I'll slink off to the lonely sidelines.

Anyhow, that's pretty much where my thoughts had brought me when Randall returned with another pint of Pilsner.

"You're doing that thing again with your teeth," he said.

"Am I? It feels good."

"Well it looks weird as hell. Like a werewolf thing."

"Half-man, half-animal. That's kind of like it, but not a wolf. A stag. I've seen images online—Pinterest paintings of forest creatures that are half-stag, half-man. Shadowy dudes with deer legs and handsome faces. And antlers. I felt this weird shiver of recognition, like maybe something like what transgender people feel. A kind of eureka moment. Like *that's* what I am."

"Stag man with a big cock."

"Do not make fun of me."

"No. I'm not here to make fun of you."

The way he said it made me ask, "Why are you here, exactly?"

He gave a little shrug, and drained a healthy chug from his pint. I pressed the point. "Is there a special reason you're here?"

"You mean did I phone you up completely by chance? No."

"Continue."

"Sylvie asked me to meet up with you. To scope you out. She's worried about you. About your deer obsession and your house looking like Exhibit A of a hoarder disorder."

"Oh really? So you fucking invite me out, loosen me up with a few pints, pry things from my mind and report back to Sylvie, is that it?" My temples were suddenly throbbing.

"That's not exactly it. Even if she hadn't asked me—look, I heard you were... Okay, how should I put this? She told me what she thought, but I didn't want to take her word for it. In fact I thought she was probably exaggerating, as women tend to do. So I wanted to check it out for myself. I was concerned."

"I'm a big boy. I can take care of myself."

"That is very funny you say that."

"Oh really?"

"She used that exact phrase when I spoke to her. Look, she still beats herself up for making a mess of your life—she knows what she did was devastating—and she's going to feel guilty about it until she sees you've got yourself together, got happy. She said she told you about that once, and you said,

'Don't flatter yourself. I'm a big boy. I'll move on.' She's not seeing that movement. I'm not seeing that movement."

That crossed a line for me. That made me furious. My fists tightened to knuckled balls. I turned away from his placid, well-meaning face, and that big elk head mounted on the wall came into view. Only the thinnest sliver of self-control kept me from bounding across the room to wreak havoc on that big old buck's massive eight-point rack. It would have felt so perfect to snap those antlers off and plunge their pointy tips into Randall's soft little eyeballs, twist them like pencils in a sharpener, and leave him bloody and sightless and vanquished, knowing he'll never again see his wife, or his kids, or the choppy waters of the Inner Harbour, or the colour blue, or anything else that can ever be seen, ever again.

Jesus Christ. Did I really think that? I did. But I didn't do it. I was just rational enough to know it wasn't Randall's fault, really. It was Sylvie's fault. *I should take this up with Sylvie. Right now.* That felt right. "You pay the bill!" I said to Randall, probably shouting it because everyone in Spinnakers stopped talking and stared at me. "Stop looking at me!" I yelled at them all, but probably they didn't understand me, because the words came out my nostrils, not my mouth. I hustled to the exit and down the metal emergency stairs, sprinting a good long way until I got winded and slowed to a walk. I walked to the Bay Street Bridge and after I crossed it, I started angling directly toward Ten Mile Point, partly on the streets and sidewalks, but often on lawns, keeping to trees and bushes, taking short cuts through unfenced back yards.

How far is it from Spinnakers to Michael's house? Maybe eight kilometres? Ten? It felt good in the cool night air to improvise a route that wasn't all right angles and cross-walks, but close to how the crow flies, or how animals move on the ground. Better in every way to be outside and free than inside, trapped across the table from some bastard who thinks he knows what's good for me. Better to be on a mission that gives purpose to the night: Stop torturing me, Sylvie, with your well-meaning concern! I'm going to put an end to all this bullshit, once and for all.

I reached Michael's house, with its grand lawn and wooded seclusion, and scaled a fence on the south side instead of going up the drive. As I got my bearings I could make out two does and two fawns checking me out. There wasn't enough streetlight to see them clearly, but I could smell them all right, and I could tell they had the same stag for their father. I just knew it from their smell. Weird, right? I just knew. I scolded their moms for doing a crap job of keeping them scent-free like they were supposed to be.

I could see the house through the trees. There was light in one ground-floor room, but otherwise it was black as charcoal. Most animals are wary of light, but it draws moths and humans. I was feeling human, like the way people say "he's only human." *Flawed*, they mean. Swagger and righteousness had carried me this far, but now I was losing it. Sobering up. Sneaking around private property in the dark.

I came sidelong to the window and peeked in. *Holy shit! HOLY SHIT!*

It's Michael's den, and there's Michael with his pants like a puddle around his feet, pumping away at Birgitta, the Danish *au pair*, who's on her elbows and bum on the desk, taking everything he's got with her legs spread straight and wide in a perfect V. He's holding her by the ankles and just pounding, really going at it, which makes me turn away from the window out of instinctive respect for their privacy, and also to collect myself, and also because seeing regular people having sex is not that attractive to look upon. I mean, Birgitta's legs are a little heavy-set, but nicely toned, but Michael, after all, is what, maybe 60? If you meet him clothed and from the front he looks very alpha male and fit, but from the back with his pants around his ankles you can see his ass is all flabby and there's varicose veins on his legs like a roadmap of Ohio. After the initial gawking from shock wears off, it's not something you want to feast your eyes on.

So I turned away into the shadow, leaning with my back against the cool, uneven stone wall of their house, thinking, Get your wits about you, Trevor. Life gets evermore complicated and then you die. What should I do? I'll make a video with my phone. That way, if and when I tell Sylvie—no need to decide for certain right now, but if I ever do tell Sylvie—she'll believe me because I will have evidence. Hard evidence. So I get my phone out and, man, that little screen is blindingly bright in the dark of night! Made me wince and squint and adjust to it before carrying out all the little preparatory steps needed to make it do my bidding—punch in password to get into it, tap photo app, slide over to video, now stick it in front of the window, staying in the shadow myself but leaning out from the wall to make sure I'm framing the action properly. *Perfect.* I press the red button and—*Shit!* The flash comes on—*Idiot!* Later I'll figure out the flash was set on manual, but how the fuck did the flash get set on manual? Likely that son of mine, that little fucker Kyle, was fucking with my phone, which wouldn't be the first time, but in the meantime, or I mean in that present moment in the dark outside Michael's mansion window, the phone is flooding light into the den and also bouncing a good percentage back off the window to illuminate my hands holding the phone, and through the glass I hear Birgitta say, "What's that?" and I'm fighting the urge to pull the phone away, because I need a proper chunk of irrefutable evidence, right? How long is irrefutable evidence? More is better than less, bravery better than cowardice. "There's a light in the window!" she squeals, and Michael is shushing her like, *Don't wake the fucking house.* He turns and looks over his shoulder toward the window, and that is my cue to pull the phone back and shut it down, and to scurry along the wall in darkness to the corner where the side of the house meets the back of the house, and then cut forty-five degrees towards the trees. Some security lights come on but there's only a second or two before I'm back in the black safety of the forest at night.

By the time I got home, the wind had picked up, and it kept me from sleeping well. The thin ends of the treetops cracked like whips, and around the houses anything not battened down rattled and clanked like Jacob Marley's chains. The couplings and crossbraces on the deer-blind next door squealed metal-on-metal like tortured cats. Deer can suffer from High Winds Panic—they get spooked by fusillades of strange noise, and hate the disorienting way the wind blasts scent at them from all directions. They can't get their bearings.

So I guess it wasn't surprising that when I woke up, Primula was snuggled right up against me. Close by, Marlene and Darlene were hunkered down uncertainly, ears atwitch. I was hung over, beer and bile taste in my mouth. A lot of saliva, like you get when you might puke. The taste made me think of Randall drinking his beer, and I imagined him reporting back to Sylvie: "You were right about Trevor. He's crossed a line: There's eccentric, there's peculiar, and then there's bat-shit crazy."

Poor Sylvie. Who's the crazy one here? She's the one living a delusion, the one whose life is about to shatter into pieces. I'm not one to obsess over my phone, but I felt for it in my pocket, feeling very protective of it. The evidence was on it. I should make a copy, or send it to my gmail or something.

Then it'll be in the cloud, and accessible from my computer, the big desktop in the rec room. So I sat up, and Primula jumped up, and in the early light of morn I watched the video clip—it was all of six seconds long, and kind of jerky and blurred—and I sent it to my gmail, and thereby to the cloud, adding six more seconds to the mountain of human stupidity documented and preserved on giant servers somewhere until the end of human civilization as we know it. Now what? What to do with it? It would be easier if I hated Sylvie. But through it all I've never hated her. *Try not to think about it, for now. I've got Primula to worry about. That's priority one.*

I went in the house to get her some morning goat milk. She followed me to the back door. She knows the drill by now: I come out with a nice bottle of slightly warmed goat milk and she guzzles it down. I left the door open, and she came close to it. She was curious, peeking inside. I shooed her back. Stay wild, little one. Stay wild. I sat on the steps while she sucked and slurped at breakfast. The wind began to drop and Darlene and Marlene got up and stretched, and wandered off.

I heard a car park in the street, and a minute later someone came into Jim and Klara's back yard. I had a clear view. A woman, thirty-something, dressed like your standard middle-class Canadian woman coming from the gym. Actually she looked a little better than that. Fit, healthy, long-legged and nimble of movement, though not petite. Five foot eight or nine, I would guess. She had on a baseball cap with her pony tail tucked through that little gap baseball caps have in the back, so her neck was exposed. I'm a sucker for a graceful neck. She went over to the blind, gripped a couple of crossbraces above the X and shook the scaffolding experimentally. The thing rattled and screeched, and Primula stopped feeding to look that way, to see what the commotion was. "Watch out for that one," I murmured. "You keep away from her, hear me?" Together we watched as she circled to the front of the blind and kicked at the peas in the bait tray. Every move she made was strong, confident, self-assured. Like a predator.

My eyes tracked her like lasers. My body became hyper-alert—every hair sprang up and stayed rigid. Sirens wailed in my head, and I held my breath like a submariner hiding from depth charges.

She bent and stirred the peas with her hand, then stood and swiveled around, doing a full 360 scope-out of her surroundings, and soon enough she spotted the two of us looking at her.

"Hey there," she called out.

Primula forgot all about her bottle and went prancing on over to meet her. I told her stop but she made a beeline for the fence and poked her nose through a diamond of the chain link, all excited, like if she pushed hard enough she could squeeze her whole body through. The huntress came to the fence and in a singsong voice said, "Look at you! What a sweetie! What are you doing, you silly? You're supposed to be off in the woods, hiding from people like me!"

I came over. Primula pulled her nose back and went running around in circles.

"What a darling. I'm Crystal," said the predator.

"Trevor."

Crystal has nice skin. It's smooth, tanned and buttery-looking. Her shoulders are muscled, like a rower's. Her breast size I'm trying to pretend is irrelevant. Trying real hard. It was noted though. Approved of.

Time to stop blabbering about what Crystal looks like (awesome), because right out of the gate Crystal and I are separated by a sea of irreconcilable differences. Start with her being the designated killer of my adopted family, my ward, my child. She wants to do it, hard as that is to believe. She signed up for it because there is profit in it.

"You're the bow-hunter?" I said.

She nodded. "Uh huh."

"You wouldn't kill a fawn, would you?"

"That depends."

"If it depends, then that's a Yes."

"Yes, then. I have killed fawns. As an act of mercy when the mother's been killed. It's hard every time. I used to keep fawns when I was a kid."

"Really?"

"Oh yeah. I grew up around animals, wild and tame." Primula came and nuzzled at the empty bottle that I held at my side. "What are you feeding her?"

"Goat milk."

"Pasteurised?"

"I guess so."

"You bought it at a grocery store?"

'Uh huh."

"Then it's pasteurised for sure. That's no good. It kills all the good bacteria."

"Oh really? What should I do?"

"Find some goat milk yogurt. Even better, find a goat farmer who'll give you milk fresh. That's what I used to do. I had three fawns all together, in three different years. They all made it through the bottle-feeding stage, so I did all right."

"Then what happened to them?"

"My dad ran them off as they got bigger. That's what he told me. I think he probably butchered them and added it to the pile of meat in the freezer, without me knowing. Not that I would have objected. I used to raise calves for 4H, and he wouldn't let me give them any name but Dinner."

"You ate your babies."

"Not my babies. Young animals I looked after for awhile. I loved them while they were alive but I learned early what gutting a deer looks like. I've been eating venison my whole life. I think it's a waste not to eat them. My dad was a taxidermist, so there was always meat around. Some hunters would pay him to butcher their kill so they could freeze it, others let us keep the meat. I grew up around hunters. There were always carcasses to dump in the back forty, and hides on the salt table."

"What's a salt table?"

"It's a taxidermy thing. Imagine a big table, maybe ten feet by ten feet, with planks on the side, and it's six inches deep with salt. That's where we would lay out the hides to dry—mostly bear hides, for making bear skin rugs."

"Wow."

"Yep. Down in the basement, where other kids had a pool table or ping pong, we had the salt table. I grew up rubbing salt into the undersides of bear hides."

"I'm on the bear's side." I said.

"I can see that. The deer's side too." She looked at Primula. "What happened to her mother?"

"Killed by a car, right out front."

She put a hand down over the fence, and Primula sniffed at it. "Poor little thing," she cooed. "Lost your mommy."

"Primula!" I said sternly. "Git! Go on, out of here." I didn't like it that she was attracted to this woman; it was like she was being suckered, lured into a trap. I bent down and grabbed her around the ribs, turned her 180, and kicked her butt gently to send her on her way.

"Wow. She's really imprinted on you. What did you do with mom?"

"I buried her here in the back yard."

"That's too bad. If I'd been around I could have helped you save some meat."

"No. I don't think I would have allowed that."

"Do you eat meat?"

"That's beside the point."

"We can agree to disagree," she said.

To say I bristled doesn't do justice to it. Every hair on my body erected and vibrated. I was a living bristle. "You are not going to kill anybody on my watch," I said.

She gave me a look like she wanted to laugh, like I was no match for her. I brought my palms up to the sides of my head because my temples suddenly stung like bee stings. Looking at her this way, her face framed by my elbows, I felt for a moment like I had antlers. My bent elbows were their pointed tips.

"I don't kill for fun," she said. "I know my place in the world, and my place in nature, which is a hell of a lot more than most people can say. Nature's out of balance. Two hundred years ago there was harmony here. Deer were here, but not in abundance—they were kept in check by prey animals like cougars and wolves. Then we showed up, Europeans I mean, and gave the First Nations people smallpox and TB, and pushed the survivors to the margins without learning anything from them about how to live here. We killed off all the cougars and wolves, and now the deer population is out of control. That's not good for nature. Look at Mount Doug Park, just beyond your property here. All the native species of trees and bushes, the Arbutus and Garry Oak especially, their young seedlings can't get established anymore. Any new growth is getting chewed to the ground or stripped bare by hordes of deer that have been allowed to proliferate, and then tough invasive foreign plants like broom and blackberries come in to fill the void. How do you fight that? I know Friends of Mount Doug organise people to go in and hack away at the broom, but that's only half the battle. To save native species we have to give them a chance to grow; we have to scale back the numbers of deer hoovering up the seedlings, and the best way to do that is either reintroduce wolves and cougars, or let people like me come in and take some deer out."

"That sounds like a well-practiced speech," I said. "You must've made it to Jim and Klara, because Klara's already parroted some of it back to me. It still doesn't justify killing deer."

"I don't have to justify it," she said. "It's all legal. The community has made a decision, democratically, with tons of input. There were tons of public meetings where you could have given your two cents worth. No one's going to come on your property and do anything you don't agree to. But over here, it's someone else's property, someone else's preference. I know what I'm doing, and I don't take it lightly. I make sure they go humanely, without suffering, with a well-placed arrow at close range. A clean kill. I've never had to chase one down to finish it off yet." She gave a shrug of uncertain meaning. Could have meant, *I'll take my leave now,* could have meant, *I'm done talking to the crazy man.* "Nice talking to you. I came by to see the homeowners," she said, and walked away.

In hindsight, there are lots of things I could have said right there and then. I can think of some good ones, in hindsight. But I just watched her walk away. Kept her hind in my sight until she reached their door.

Stealth is a quality I admire more and more. Especially in myself. When exposure can get you killed, it's better to stay hidden. It's not cowardice, it's common sense. To be able to move about in the world without a sound, so that you see all, yet are not seen: That's an awesome quality to have.

Crystal was knocking on Jim and Klara's back door. I went back in my house, darted up the stairs to the glass door of my deck and slid it open, like, stealthily. On my belly I slithered silently to the far edge of the deck with its perfect view of their back yard. I kept hidden behind the line of tomato plants in their big pots. The top edges of the pots touched each other but the bottoms tapered away, creating a triangular gap between. Perfect cover to peek through and listen as Crystal talked technique with them.

She told them she was going to set up a camera triggered by a motion detector, let it run for a few days, and that way pinpoint what time the deer came to feed at the bait station. "They're very regular," she said. "They have a nightly route around their territory that they stick to like clockwork. So what'll happen is, I'll check the camera for a couple of days and get a bead on the time they show up here, and then on the third day I'll come a bit early, climb up into the blind, and—"

"Boom!" Jim crowed. "Goodbye deer!"

"Not boom," she said. "This is bow-hunting, remember?"

"Right. Silent but deadly!"

Even at a distance, up on the deck, I could tell she was not impressed with Jim's enthusiasm. It was clear from her body language, in the way she turned her head slightly, like you do to avoid a bad smell. It was super subtle, so he wouldn't have noticed—just the slightest chink in the armour of her "Customer is always right" exterior, with its semi-fake smile.

I actually felt something like admiration for her in that moment, even though I thought of her as a predator, and Darlene, Marlene, and Primula as her defenseless prey. Not totally defenseless—they have me on their team. I felt she was a worthy opponent, and that our predator–prey interface was in keeping with nature. There's no free will in nature. Animals are born to live out their predestined roles. There is something predestined about the looming battle between Crystal and me. It's fated that the winner will be the cleverest, the most ingenious, the most wily. If it was only Crystal versus the girls, it's obvious who would win. They'd be frigging venison by lunchtime. But this time they have a ringer in their corner. Me.

At my session with Rolanda today I was eager to get some advice on the best way to stop Crystal from killing my family. I had a bunch of questions ready to go. Should I shut off that camera Crystal set up to track their feeding times? Or better yet, steal it? Empty the bait station? Tie a rope to the blind and tip it over? Unfortunately I never got that far, because Rolanda, in her gentle, non-confrontational way, was right from the get-go determined to steer our conversation away from anything concrete and useful like saving the lives of innocent animals. Before I'd even got comfortable, she said, "If you don't mind, I'd like to go back to where we left off last time. You were just telling me how Sylvie made it known she was leaving."

"Right! Sylvie!" I said. "I have a bunch of questions I need to ask you, but also something has happened with Sylvie, and I was going to tell you, but then I met Crystal and it's like my brain can only operate on a single track right now. Juggling two things is like straining under too much weight—ever seen a weightlifter like in the Olympics fall down and almost get crushed by the weights? My brain feels like that—I went out with my old buddy Randall for beers, and it turns out Sylvie set him up to snoop on me—"

"Why would she do that?"

"Because she cares. Because she thinks I'm getting weird."

"Do you think you're getting weird?"

"That's beside the point. I have to tell you something." Something had distracted me—some scent I detected in the room. I took a deep breath, and then another, then my nostrils flared wide as bellbottoms, and in one massive snort I inhaled about a cubic metre of air.

"You're ovulating," I said.

"Pardon me?"

"Sorry. It just came out. I breathed it. Sensed it."

"Sensed it how?"

"With all my senses, but mostly smell. I have a super-heightened sense of smell. I can differentiate between smells, even. Like for example, within the last few days someone used vinegar and water to clean the windows."

"Wow. Interesting."

"Yeah. Like a Jacobson's organ," I said. She looked puzzled, so I explained to her how deer sort smells with it. I was sitting with my legs splayed on the floor in that half-swastika posture I find comfortable these days, with my arms on the seat of one of her comfy chairs, and now I pulled myself up. A deep intake of breath brought my attention back to a whole bouquet of smells, dominated by the one announcing Rolanda's heightened state of fertility. The odour came to me right through her clothes.

"Now is the best possible day for you to conceive," I said.

Her eyes went saucer-wide for a sec, then she pulled herself back into unflusterable, non-judgemental therapist mode. "Thank you, Trevor," she said firmly. By which she meant, Enough, Trevor.

"It just slipped out! Sorry if it freaks you out."

"It does. The strange part is, you're right. I've been keeping track lately because my partner and I are trying to have a child."

"Great. Wonderful. Kids are great. How long have you been at it?"

"A little while. Not long enough to be worried, but getting there."

I got excited and said, "Here's a technique that might help, once you're in bed and getting ready to go: Get him to crouch down behind you and make a fawn face, like a puppy or kitten face, and have him make cute little meowing noises. Peek at him over your shoulder while he does that and your maternal instincts will get stimulated for sure!"

"Thank you, Trevor," she said again. Same meaning as last time. Then came an awkward silence, which is to be expected, considering I'd just coaxed her to do it doggy style like every other land mammal does, except maybe kangaroos, I'm not up on marsupials. Something else was happening. Remember I told you my cock is getting bigger and thicker? Encouraged by thoughts of shapely and well endowed Rolanda getting it doggy-style, my cock was pulsing with emanations of—how to describe it? The sex signal, straight from penis to brain. Greedy, needy, craving, aching, voracious, rapacious, whatever human words exist will all be found insufficient to describe the way my cock swelled, pulsated and strained insistently, pinned down in my pants like Gulliver among the Lilliputians. To be fully honest, it overwhelmed my mind and made me imagine it was *me* serving Rolanda, *me* fully committed to the rut, and why not? I felt potent, virile—to hell with her old man, whoever he was! I'd drag him off her, send him packing with a mighty head butt, and set myself to plowing the furrow! I should be the one to plant the seed! Rolanda was looking at me funny and because of the thoughts I was having I got self-conscious and dropped my eyes and couldn't look at her, and then for some reason I pictured Michael pounding away at Birgitta in his den in the dark forest, and I thought, I should be the one pounding away at Birgitta! I don't have varicose veins! My ass is way less saggy than his!

t felt—sheesh—some part of me feels embarrassed to go on and on about it, but I have to say it: At that exact moment the exact center of the universe was in the head of my cock. I am serious: Energy flooded towards me from every direction as the universe aligned itself and sped and fed into an evermore intense spiral, spinning and sucking all the colliding random forces of light and dark matter into an ever-tighter vortex that merged with pinpoint precision in the epicenter of my pants. I had a hard-on. Every man knows what that feels like when it appears unbidden of its own accord and duels with rationality and the social contrivances like etiquette and shit that are the bedrock of our civilization. Every man knows what that feels like. Well multiply that feeling by a million, or a billion. Women on the other hand can't possibly know what that feels like, to be possessed by that feeling. It's not an *intentional* feeling, I didn't *will* it, or create it, or even ask for it. It was bestowed upon me by the universe, for better or worse. Anyway, I don't think in that time and place Rolanda noticed that the entirety of the universe was converging in my pants—I was wearing an untucked flannel shirt, and I think there was coverage. It was taut and hurt like an overstretched sausage straining not to burst its skin— of course it hurt! It was primordial but my highly socialized human mind fought it, scolded it, like, DO YOU KNOW

*HOW MUCH TROUBLE YOU COULD GET ME INTO?
I NEED TO TAKE YOU OUTSIDE—LET'S GET THE
HELL OUT OF HERE!*

Meanwhile sweet kindly Rolanda did her best to gently
nudge me back on track. "You were telling me about your
friend Randall, that you went out for beers with," she said
encouragingly. Right. So I picked up the thread of my story
of Randall at Spinnakers, getting increasingly enthusiastic
as I described trekking halfway across town to Michael's
mansion in the dark and then making that clandestine video
of the old master and young servant fucking their brains out
with gusto but at the same time doing it furtively so as not to
wake the lady of the house. By the time I was done spinning
the tale to Rolanda I was winded, all out of breath, with just
enough left in me to sputter, "So now we know he's cheating
on Sylvie, and I've got the goods to prove it, so what do I
do? Do I tell her, Rolanda? How do I tell her?"

Rolanda looked very troubled. "Let's backtrack a bit," she
said. "There are implications to some of your actions here,
that I'm not sure you're appreciating. For example: In the
middle of the night, you went onto someone else's property
and shot video through their window?"

"Yee-es."

"Trevor, don't you think that's a bit outside the realm of
normal behaviour? I think it's safe to say it's illegal, even.
And likely that makes the video illegal."

"I don't care," I said. "Legal, illegal—that's just an artificial construct. A human construct. The deer I saw in the

woods in the night over there, they don't know or care about that. They don't bother with No Trespassing signs."

"Trevor, we are not deer."

"I know. I know that. But the end justifies the means, right? When a superhero breaks into the bad guy's lair no one says, wait a minute, that's trespassing. He's doing what's right!"

"Can I get you to agree on something?" she asked. "We are not deer, and we're not superheroes either. We're just people, trying to make sense of things. Think of your actions last night. Ask yourself whether they're impulsive, and where the impulses are coming from."

"Spiral emanations from the center of the universe," I explained, trying to sound reasonable.

"Pardon?"

Odd thing to say, I know. It was like my cock was verbalizing. Or I was translating what my cock was feeling. In no way had its painful intensity subsided while I'd nattered on so civilized-like about Michael and Birgitta. It was still there, demanding to explode out of my pants, taking over my body and mind until there was nothing for it but to leap up, sputtering *Thank you Thank you Thank you* for no clear reason and then bounding toward the door and out it and gone without so much as a goodbye, or setting up the next appointment, or any of the usual human pleasantries. So happy to get out and away! That was weird! I was really not in control. I drove back out to Gordon's Head with one hand on the steering wheel and one hand on my jeans taking the measure of that insistent cock. *Take it easy, boy, take it easy!* You would think when I got home, got inside, out of sight and all private-like, that the first thing I'd do is give it the relief it so craved, and in fact I was dying to do that in the car so bad it made shifting gears a challenge, but when I did get home and alone in the house, some stronger and stranger impulse in me cried out, *NO NO NO NO NO Trevor! DO not WASTE it!!! That is ONLY to be PUT in its PROPER PLACE!!!!*

I need some down time. I need to go feed Primula and satisfy myself she's okay, then I need to fall asleep.

I got her mix of goat milk and yogurt ready in a bottle and went out and called "Primula!" Usually she sticks close to the house, because she knows that's home base. I may go away but I always come back. So far she hasn't tried to follow me when I drive the car. I worry about that, that she might start doing that. Anyhow I called and called, and no Primula. I looked around in the back with unease growing and a bad taste in my mouth. I kept spitting saliva out, like marking my territory. No sign of her in back. I went out to the street and looked up and down, trying to decide what direction to go. A woman came along with a little lap dog on a leash; she'd done up its hair into a topknot tied with a ribbon, bobbing above its tiny skull, utterly stupid and ridiculous. I hate it when people dress up dogs, it's so demeaning and not what dogs are about, but being Canadian I said she looks cute like that. The exact opposite of what I was thinking. She said it's not a she it's a he and that made me hate the ribbon even more, because I'm old school and unprogressive when it comes to males wearing ribbons in their hair, be it dogs or teenagers experimenting with their sexual identity. I know it shouldn't matter, it's just a ribbon and not a signifier of gender but this is not the time to worry about that, all I want to say is rather than walking around looking all cutesy, that dog would rather be flushing rats from their holes and ripping their little heads off. I could see he had the ideal teeth and personality for ratting because he came full speed at my ankles like a yappy little bantamweight and the woman had to yank the leash full force to keep him from ripping my pants. I kicked at him, wishing I had razor-sharp hooves rather than rubber-soled Keens. She scolded him, apologized to me and said, "He's all agitated because we saw the cutest little fawn in someone's flowers, just up the street there."

At the word "fawn" I took off like a shot and sure enough there was Primula about eight houses up, munching away in someone's front garden. It was one of those well-tended gardens, almost like you see in magazines, except too orderly, too regimented—in the magazines they always look tended and yet natural at the same time, but this one was over-tended, almost Fascistic in its perfect order, and there was Primula standing in a bed of pink and purple foxglove, sniffing at it and taking tentative nibbles of the smaller, newer, upper leaves. "Foxglove! Jesus Fucking Christ," I yelled. "What the *hell* are you doing Primula?? That shit'll kill you!!!"

I shooed her out of there and she pranced and kicked happily around me. I examined the plants, trying to gauge how much she'd ingested. There were places where leaves were lacking. Had she eaten them off? Hard to say. Maybe they just hadn't grown in there yet. By the time we got home and I had her settled down on the back steps, she was not looking her usual frisky self, in fact she was starting to look downright quavery and wavery on her feet.

I was furious with myself for... for... Well really, it's not my fault. I can't blame myself, I'm doing my best—she doesn't have a proper deer mother to steer her clear of dangerous food. I should blame those fucking gardeners up the street, nourishing their toxic killer plants. I told myself, Tonight when the (human) world sleeps I'm going to super-stealthily swing by that house and yank every last foxglove out by the roots! But that's for later. Meanwhile I was looking at Primula and thinking, Holy shit, she's eaten foxglove and she's going to die unless I get some activated charcoal into her.

I'd done my due diligence you see, after Mike from Saanich Pound said lots of baby fawns die from eating foxglove. I'd googled it, read up on it, paying particular attention to antidotes. All the info was re: how to save humans, not a word about saving deer, but I figured, Humans, deer, we're all mammals right? And for humans the best strategy is absorption—i.e. the walls of the stomach don't absorb things very well compared to something like activated charcoal, which absorbs things like crazy. In the case of foxglove ingestion, if you eat activated charcoal then all the digitalis poison absorbs into the activated charcoal, and binds to it until it passes right through you and you shit it out. So I figured I needed activated charcoal and clicked on how to get activated charcoal, and you know what google said step one was? Make charcoal. The Source of All Knowledge was not being helpful there, but eventually I figured out I didn't need to make my own, you can just buy activated charcoal at the pharmacy in convenient pill form. So I'd bought some, just in case. I was proud of that—of being such a proactive parent that I actually had activated charcoal on hand.

Dairy products are also very absorbent, so I ground up a couple of activated charcoal pills, dumped them in the bottle with the goat milk and goat yogurt and shook it up real good. By this time Primula was sitting on the bottom step looking downright woozy. I got the bottle in her mouth but she wasn't sucking on it, so I took the lid off and tried to pour it down her throat. Under normal circumstances it would have been impossible to get her to hold still, but this time she was docile and compliant. She was kind of droopy. The milk mixture was running down her lower jaw and neck, but some of it was getting swallowed. I think. Hard to tell. I was coaxing her to take it when someone called out, "You all right over there?"

It was Crystal, at the fence.

"Not exactly. She ate some foxglove. I'm trying to get the antidote into her."

"You want some help?"

I looked at her for a minute, thinking: *This is the enemy. The enemy wants to help.* It surprised me what came out of my mouth: "Sure."

So that's how Crystal ended up on my back steps with me, holding Primula in her arms and massaging her little chest and throat. She kept muttering to her in a cooing baby voice—like, "You are so cute, look at you, little one! I love your spots!" I was thinking similar thoughts about Crystal, only substitute the word tits for spots. Highly relevant. That is one good-looking, perfectly-proportioned woman. So fine, so fit, as befits a huntress, a predator, which given who she wants to hunt and predatorize, I shouldn't like so much, and I do hate that part of her, but the rest I find difficult to hate.

In fact I like it a lot. I put the nipple back on the bottle and my little girl took it and sucked on it, not with gusto, but at least she got some of it into her. I explained to Crystal about activated charcoal, and she said, "What about when she chews her cud? Are you going to try to get her to spit it out before she re-swallows?"

"I didn't think of that. Making her spit out her cud would likely traumatize her for life. She probably has some reflex, like the opposite of a gag reflex, that makes it almost impossible to spit out. Hopefully the toxins stay bound to the charcoal even when she re-chews."

"I'm not even sure she's in the cud-chewing stage yet—that comes when she's eating leaves and grasses," said Crystal.

"She's always turned up her nose at the salad greens I bought her," I said. "Foxglove is the first green thing I've seen her eat." To Primula I scolded, "You little fool."

"But right now her diet is still mostly goat milk, right?" said Crystal. "Did you get her some yogurt?"

"I did. Thank you."

Primula turned her head away from the bottle like she was full, and wandered off unsteadily to sit in the tall grass. Crystal stood up and said, "See you later, sweetie." To Primula, not to me. Obviously. She has beautiful skin. I know, I said it before. Smooth and buttery. A scent filled my head.

"You smell good," I said.

"What?"

"Mango and aloe vera shampoo, am I right?"

"I'd have to think about that." She touched her hair, ran her fingers through it like a comb, as if that might help her remember. "I think you're right, actually. But I haven't washed it in two days."

"I was going to say that. It's not freshly washed, but traces linger."

"Quite the nose you have," she said.

"I think it's from looking after baby here. I'm getting deer senses. Heightened smell for sure." As if to demonstrate I sucked some major air up my nose, and I wasn't expecting to be overwhelmed, but there you go—my head spun from an onslaught of odours and I almost said something even more stupid and socially inappropriate than "You smell good." I almost said, "By my reckoning you'll ovulate in two to three days," because I knew it was true just by taking a long, deep whiff of the oxygen, nitrogen, and assorted other molecules swirling in and around lovely Crystal, that creature of human contradiction who was so happy to help me nurse my baby, but also happy to kill her.

It is strange and new that my nose speaks to me. There is meaning to smell but no words, so I can't write them down. My cock is also talking. At that moment it did not engorge and grow or otherwise put me at risk of outward embarrassment, but inwardly it pulsated like a drumbeat and trumpeted loud and clear: *If I encounter Crystal two to three days from now, there will be no stopping me. It'll be: "Get Out of my Way, Trevor."*

Primula stood up, straggled a step or two, and started to poop. "I should wipe her bum," I said.

"Really? You do that?"

"Yeah. It's what the moms do in nature. They put their mouths right down there and catch it and eat it, and afterwards they lick the bums clean. I draw the line at a wet facecloth."

"That is hilarious. I never did that with any of my fawns."

"It protects her from predators, so they won't smell her. I'm trying to keep her wild as I can. You probably kept yours in a barn, or a shed or something."

"That's right, I did. I had to keep our dogs away from them. Look at her—she's trying to lick her own ass."

"Primula! Don't! You'll put the poison back in your mouth, you silly!"

I said it scoldingly enough that my raised voice startled her and she skittered off under the gnarled branches of the Garry Oaks, still within sight. She was looking better. I felt a load lift from my heart.

"She's so cute," said Crystal.

"You couldn't really kill her, could you?" I said.

"No. I don't think I could, now," she said. "I've gotten to know her a little too well."

"Promise me you won't."

She ran a finger along her lower lip, thinking. When she raised her eyes I saw tenderness in them. "I promise," she said. "But try to keep her out of Jim's yard. If I'm in the blind and they see her come wandering over to feed they'll be super mad if I don't pull the trigger."

"Trigger? I thought it was a bow and arrow."

"Crossbow. The better weapon in a confined space."

"Huh. What about Marlene and Darlene? You're still planning on killing them?"

"If they come within range, I'm afraid I'll have to. It's business, unfortunately. I've got obligations to meet—I only ask for half the fee upfront. There're lots of expenses. To get full payment I need a result."

"But they're young," I said. "They were born last year. They're adolescents, really."

She shook her head. "Sorry. I'm invested now, as far as time and money goes. No harvest, no reward."

"For a minute I thought you had a heart."

"I have half a heart. I've caved on Primula." She stood before me and stretched like a sleek cat, like an athlete, palms raised to heaven, face to the sun. So lovely I could hardly look at her. "I've gotta go," she said. "Gotta have a look at the camera and figure out prime time. I'm a woman of my word, so you can rest easy knowing Primula will get to grow up. I'll let Sky know—no fawns. Spare the fawn."

"Sky?"

"He works for me. I've got plans this weekend—my best friend's getting married and the bachelorette party's Saturday night—so Sky will be on duty."

"Saturday, that's your target date? What's that, two nights from now?"

"Is it? Holy crumoli, time's flying. Is today Thursday already? I better get on over there. Got to pinpoint the feeding schedule so we don't sit in the blind all night."

"So it might be Sky doing the killing?"

"Culling, not killing. We call it 'culling,' or 'harvesting.' It's not about slaughter. I'm actually strengthening the herd."

"I'll let Darlene and Marlene know that. They'll feel so much better."

She didn't say anything.

"I'll keep my eye out for Sky," I said.

"What do you mean?"

"I'll be looking after my girls."

"By doing what?"

"Whatever it takes."

Our eyes met. There was no hint of that tenderness I'd seen when she promised to spare Primula. This was predator–prey. She's the wolf, I'm the shepherd. My temples felt like missile silos opening. I had to close my eyes and cradle my face. I wished I had antlers to drive her away. Also, believe it or not, for some reason I thought antlers would impress her.

"Let's keep it peaceful," she said. "I promised about Primula. You need to promise you'll keep it peaceful."

"I'm not the predator here," I said. "Everything I do is in self-defence."

"Just stay on your side of the fence."

"We'll see."

"I'm going to tell Sky about Primula, but I should also warn him about you," she said.

"Whatever. I'm sure he'll be a worthy opponent."

That's how we left it. She headed over to the camera in Jim and Klara's backyard and wrote down some readings off it. I watched her. On her way out she waved to me, like a friendly wave, and she called out "Bye Primula." My little fawn tippy-toed merrily over to the fence to meet her. Crystal put a hand out and she licked it.

"The charcoal must be working," she said.

I nodded, and caught her scent. I hate that she's a huntress, but man, I love the way she smells.

I'm waiting for nightfall so I can go rip out those foxglove up the street, and to pass the time while I keep an eye on Primula I'm scribbling in this journal in the back yard. I can tell you something—I'm seeing blue super brightly these days. I've noticed that. I'm seeing right off the scale into ultra-violet. On the other end of the spectrum, reds and yellows and oranges are all fading into pale shadows of their former selves.

What does it mean to see colours, anyway? Reality is limited and defined by biology. That's it. Reality is changing for me, but it's gradual, so I'm not shocked. I adapt, and what is different becomes normal. What is "seeing"? Strictly speaking it's the perception of electromagnetic wavelengths bouncing off objects. What is "colour"? Our brains differentiating tiny variations in these wavelengths. Colour doesn't exist except as categories in our minds. If I close my eyes I can still imagine red, but stop signs when I'm driving are kind of a yellowish grey to me now. I still see them, that's the main thing. I'm still a mammal. You know how much of the electromagnetic spectrum humans can see? One ten-trillionth. I learned it on PBS. That show about the brain. I've got a mind for stats like that. Good at trivia. One-ten-trillionth! The point is we see a tiny fraction of reality, just enough so we don't bump into chairs. Deer see ultraviolet light, so they see a bit more at the top end. I'm starting to see it too. Let me tell you, it is bright! It radiates! It fucking glows! That's why they put it in laundry detergent, did you know about that? They add chemicals to reflect ultra-violet light so your clothes look cleaner than they are. They're no cleaner but they're brighter, sucker! Humans and crows—we love our shiny objects.

You know who has a ton of ultraviolet reflectors in their feathers? Hummingbirds. There's a rufous hummingbird pair that live in the thicket. When I first started sleeping out in the back yard, they used to come and visit me a lot in the morning, I think because I have a red sleeping bag. They love red, which is why hummingbird feeders have red plastic flowers at the bottom. The male has an amazing patch of shiny feathers on his throat and chest; it's iridescent, and he can even aim it like a mirror, and reflect a beam of light from it to illuminate something he wants to see better, like the shadowed stigma of an ovary hidden deep inside a long-petaled flower. I love watching my hummingbird friends at work. Since I've started bedding down outdoors, I'm part of their world, it feels like. They come and borrow bits of lint from around the edges of the dryer vent on the back of the house, and carry it away to make their nests. I say "borrow" because they do give back, in the pleasure of watching them buzz around the place. I've seen one drive off a Cooper's Hawk, no problem.

They're feisty, they fight a lot among themselves, hum-mingbirds do. Just now they were flitting in and out of the thicket like a re-enactment of the Battle of Britain when some movement back there caught my eye. Darlene and Marlene coming home? Maybe. In fact yes, they were, I smelled them for sure before I saw them for sure. But there was a third smell too, another deer, but not a deer, more complicated than a deer is what I can say, another creature giving off a mix of smells I couldn't sort, and I had a funny feeling I was being watched. I felt my hairs stand up. Something was there, and watching me, and it felt supernatural, is all I can say. Charlene's ghost? *Can a ghost have a smell? No. This thing is alive.* Or was it? An apparition? I thought I caught a glimpse. A woman? A doe? A woman of the woods. I called out, "Come here where I can see you, Woman of the Woods!" Is she just coy? A tease? Is she really there? Is she real?

I need sleep. A catnap will do me good, get me ready for stealth gardening tonight.

I have so many things to say, I feel it's important to write everything down now, in case there's trouble later. I get the feeling big trouble is coming. First off there's the video of Michael with his drawers dropped, boffing Birgitta on his desk. Rolanda didn't help by telling me it's illegal, but that's a minor annoyance—what weighs more heavily is what to do with it. Show it to Sylvie? Send it anonymously to her somehow? Does she need the heartache? Is she better off not knowing? What's the best outcome here? Best outcome should be the least suffering for everyone involved. Let's aim for that.

The best outcome would be for Michael to clean up his act and become a true and devoted partner, right? In that scenario Sylvie doesn't necessarily even ever have to know. That scenario can be accomplished by confronting *him*, not her. He can get sorted and she can remain unharmed and blissfully unaware, right? He's probably all off-kilter and ill-at-ease right now, knowing someone's got the goods on him, waiting for the shoe to drop. I could let him know that someone is *me*, and make it clear I'm not trying to blackmail him, I'm just aiming to extract a promise of good behaviour going forward. Keep your nose clean, keep to the straight and narrow, or else Sylvie gets a private screening of *Horndog Mike's Midnight Madness*. Would that even work? Even if he promised, how would I monitor him?

All these thoughts kept me from sleep. I didn't sleep even a second before the alarm on my phone went off at 2 a.m. I'd set it so I could get up and pull foxgloves up the street. In the cool still quiet of night Primula followed along, traipsing hither and yon over the lawns while I stuck to the pavement. This is suburbia—there are no sidewalks. About five houses down, we met up with Darlene and Marlene, who are almost grown up and therefore know better than to chow down on foxglove. How do they learn that? I don't know, and I can't ask them. Which is frustrating, although more and more I feel like we communicate without words on the important things. They followed along behind and when the four of us got there I did my stealthy ninja imitation, slipping up the side of the house to avoid the motion detector mounted above the front door, then doubling back into the foxglove patch, which was a dozen or so plants.

I hadn't brought a shovel or anything—I was just going to grab 'em by the stalks and pull 'em out roots and all, and it was working out pretty good, I had a neat little pile of eight or nine leafy stalks laid out straight when Primula danced across the lawn and tripped the motion detector, and the world was suddenly fucking blindingly bright with light as pure as the gates of heaven. "Jesus Fucking Christ," I muttered, or at least I should have muttered but instead said it kind of loud. Not cool. *Oh well, three plants to go, let's hurry and get the hell out of here.* I was bent over the last plant giving it a mighty and satisfying heave when the front door was opened by a pajama-clad older dude with a kitchen knife in his hand, I kid you not. Armed and dangerous, except he was too old to come across as super-dangerous, because I could always just turn tail and outrun him. "What the hell are you doing on my property?" he shouted.

Property! I am so sick of that word! My first impulse was to say, "Shhh! You'll wake the neighbours." The world holds its breath in the silent seconds after people shout in the quiet night. Primula and the two older girls were riveted to the spot. Eventually words came out of my mouth. "These plants are poisonous to deer and need to be removed."

"Poisonous to deer? I don't give a tinker's damn! You get off my property right now!"

"I'm going, I'm going," I said. I dropped the last of the plants onto the leafy sheaf on the ground, bent down and scooped up the whole bunch in my arms, and did my best to casually saunter away. Not running, that would look like I'd done something wrong. He called after me, "Wait! I know you! You live up the street!"

I switched gears, took it up a notch to speed-walking. I glanced behind me and he was coming down the steps to his lawn, shouting, "I canvassed your house—for the Heart and Stroke Foundation! I know you!"

Jesus Christ. I was now officially running, straight for home. I could hear him behind calling out for me to stop. I sprinted up the driveway, through the carport into the backyard and into the thicket. "When in doubt, hide in the thicket," that's my new motto. Marlene, Darlene, and Primula were right there with me, in fact they went further back into the shadows than I did. I lingered along the edge where I could peek out and see if we were being followed. No. All was quiet, and the night returned to silence, with only the faintest insect hum of a faulty streetlamp eighty yards away, and the soft sound of traffic further in the distance.

Crap! What do I do? I couldn't crouch there all night. After a while I took the foxglove and scrunched and folded the long stocks up and tamped them into the compost bin, then went into the house to use the toilet. Sitting there with my pants around my ankles I had the urge to bite my nails—my toe nails. I don't think I've ever wanted to do that before but now I did and I was even able to bring them up to my mouth, which I don't think I ever had the flexibility to do either. I was nibbling at them, trying to make them sharp. Razor sharp. They seem thicker these days and biting them was hard, even as I tried to get them deep into my mouth, back to those big new molars I have back there. They didn't reach so I decided I'd need a knife or scissors to do the job right, but before that the door bell rang. Never good when the doorbell rings at three in the morning.

I got off the throne and hitched up my pants and opened the front door to come face to face with two of Saanich's finest, amiable enough looking guys once I got over the uniform. One was a boozer—I could smell his sweat, it reeked of yesterday's bender. He was sober now. Both guys smelled over-caffeinated and a bit stressed, presumedly from previous encounters in their evening of keeping the peace. From the get-go, I told myself to stay polite and reasonable, and don't deny anything, just come across as some middle-aged suburban dude who'd plucked a few plants from a garden. That would make a nice break for them from the drunks, car crashes and domestic violence they see all too often. Make them like me. Piece of cake.

"You guys are quick," I said.

"It's a slow night," said the drinker. "We hear someone's been picking flowers."

"Foxglove. That plant should be illegal. It's highly poisonous, guys."

"Is it?"

"Oh yeah! It'll kill a deer, especially a fawn who doesn't know any better."

"Okay then," he nodded. Nice—we seemed to be on the same page. Then he asked, "But is it a good idea to tear it out of a neighbour's garden without discussing with him first?"

"He would've said no. He would've said get lost. I was performing a public service, is how I see it. Acting for the public good." *Perfect. Nice and reasonable.*

"The law doesn't see it that way," the cop said. "The law says you've done something you shouldn't."

That got my blood stirring.

The other cop said, from memory, "Everyone who, without lawful excuse, the proof of which lies on him, loiters or prowls at night on the property of another person near a dwelling-house situated on that property, is guilty of an offence punishable on summary conviction."

He looked very pleased with himself.

My head started to throb. I was rocking back and forth on my feet. I put my hands up above my temples, and through the hair I could feel the skin was splitting, on both sides. Something was trying to push its way up and out, like tree roots coming through pavement. My fingers were bloody, but just a little, and the blood was sticky, brownish, half-dried.

"Are you alright?" asked the boozer.

"Yeah. I'm having some health issues right now."

"Do you have meds for it?"

"No."

"You don't have meds or you're just not taking them?"

"I don't want or need meds!" It came out way too loud. I corrected the volume. "Sorry. I'm fine, really. You think I'm bipolar or something, probably."

"We're not medical professionals. But I would recommend if you're not seeing one already, you seek one out. I think we can all agree, your behaviour tonight is a bit beyond normal."

"I'm in therapy. With Rolanda." I don't know why I said her name. They wouldn't know her.

"Good. That's a start. I tell you what. We're going to leave charges at this time. However, any further incidents and we'll revisit the need for charges to be laid."

I dabbed a Kleenex near my temples. "Okay, good. Thank you officers."

"Right now we're going to go back up the street and talk to your neighbour." He looked me straight in the eye. "Is there anything you'd like us to tell him?"

"Tell him he almost killed Primula."

The two cops exchanged a glance like, *Shit, here we go.*

"I beg your pardon?"

"His fucking foxglove almost killed my little fawn."

"We'll pass that along. But don't you think, also, an apology would be in order? You gave the old guy quite a scare there, waking him up like that, well after midnight."

Why did they have to bring him up? Thinking of that old fucker made me wish I'd had a chance to get my toe nails nice and sharp. Then I thought, Get a grip, Trevor.

"Yeah, okay. I get it. Tell him I'm sorry," I said, amazed at the human capacity to lie.

"Good then. We'll pass that along. And we'll tell him you're going to stay put for the rest of the night."

"Yes, yes. I got all the foxglove, so there's no reason to go back."

"We'll just tell him you promised you won't bother him anymore."

Their cop car was on the street right in front of the house, broadcasting a low-volume stream of bleeps and short comments from a radio dispatcher. As they headed to it, Jim came out of his house and met them just as they were getting in. Why Jim was awake at three in the morning I can't say for sure—maybe he's having trouble sleeping ever since I terrorized him the other day. He leaned in at the passenger side window and spoke to the cops for some time. Saying what? I can only imagine. Probably it was along the lines of "Trevor tried to head-butt me and left blood upon my back door." Probably they would add it to my file and reconsider laying charges. *Fuck!* That tight-ass Jim was leaning into the car in such a way that his tight ass presented a perfect target to me, and I had to fight an urge to lower my head and sprint the thirty feet or so between us, and ram him hard, which would have felt fantastic. I could have launched him through the window like a human torpedo onto the laps of Saanich's finest. I fought that urge and won. I went inside and sharpened my toenails.

I was having a dream about Kyle being a baby again and being very sick, swollen and bloated, covered with spots like measles, and Sylvie and I were living like homeless people on the streets of some city that could have been Montreal. The dream had a deep feeling of despair, hopelessness and unsolvability. Then Kyle was calling "Dad, wake up!" and shaking my shoulder and I woke up in the back yard, with him and Sylvie looking at me. They looked kind of grossed out and disgusted by me, and I think Kyle even said "Eeewww," the unfiltered way kids say it. I wiped at the side of my mouth—a river of drool had leaked out and flowed down over the crook of my elbow—a bit disgusting to them maybe but not me, what the hell, it's all natural.

"Where are the girls?" I said.

"Good morning," said Sylvie.

"What's going on?" I said.

"Kyle left some books here, we came to get them."

"For my project," said Kyle. "Remember, aerodynamics?"

I didn't, but said, "Okay."

"I hear there was all kinds of activity around here last night," said Sylvie. "Klara texted me."

I rubbed my head above the temples and felt the bumps. My fingertips came away clean. The blood had dried.

"Tell Klara to mind her own fucking business," I said.

"Trevor! Your son is here."

"Dad swears all the time," said Kyle. "We're used to it."

"Not all the time," I said. "When warranted."

"Spare me your platitudes!" Kyle shouted, in a Darth Vader voice.

"What?" I said.

"Nothing," said Sylvie. "Kyle, smarten up."

"That's what Michael says when he imitates you, Dad," Kyle said. "It sounds funny. 'Spare me your platitudes!'" Again with that Darth Vader intonation.

"I've never said that in my life," I said.

"Oh you did," said Sylvie. "The first time you met him."

I stood up, too abruptly. In my half-asleep state it was tough to get my feet under me. Thinking back to that first meeting with Michael, I do remember him spouting all kinds of crap about how love can't be tamed, or controlled, or mapped out, and how you have to let it meander like a river and find its own course and how everything will always work out for the best if love is granted its freedom or some such platitudinous bullshit, so it's quite possible I did get fed up and told him to Spare Me His Platitudes.

"So now I'm comic fodder over at Michael's place," I said. "Great to know I'm the glue that holds the new family together."

"It's not like that," said Sylvie.

"I really don't give a fuck," I said. This time she did not scold me about swearing in front of our kid. Was he really our kid? I felt very little for him, and not much for Sylvie either because she had finished ovulating about a week ago— don't ask me how I know that because I've already told you

I have Super Smell now, and I'm already used to it and think it's normal. The new normal. Anyhow I said to Sylvie, "Do you remember a while back—we were watching some PBS documentary on the brain, and they were talking about how the male mind can unconsciously perceive when a female is ovulating?"

"No," she said.

"Come on! I'm pretty sure we saw it together—that series on the brain, hosted by that guy Eagleman or whatever. And he was talking about how lap-dancers earn double in tips when they're ovulating as compared to when they're menstruating. The clients don't consciously know where the women are in their cycle, but unconsciously they do."

"I think I vaguely remember that," she said. "And?"

"Well—actually, nothing. Forget it." Maybe it wasn't the moment to discuss her cycle and my heightened perception of it. But I had a fleeting thought that maybe the fact she was done ovulating last week explained Michael's actions this week.

"Spare me your platitudes!" Kyle crowed yet again.

This time I felt less than zero familial bond with that little fucker, mocking his old man like that, right to my face. Is that natural? Maybe it is. Maybe it's like those nature docs where the old patriarch in the baboon pack gets bloodied and driven off by his own son. No loyalty there. Nature in all its crowning cruelty. I had an urge to be cruel to Kyle, the little turncoat, in fact I had a severe urge to knock him on his ass and trample him. I didn't though. I'm proud of myself for that, that I spared the child. Instead I followed another urge: to locate Primula and assure myself she wasn't getting up to any clueless foolishness like eating foxglove or prancing up to pit bulls. "Where's Primula?" I said.

"We saw her!" Kyle said. "She's over there, in Jim and Klara's back yard."

"What the fuck, why didn't you tell me?"

I didn't wait for an answer—in a flash I bounded to the fence, leapt it like nothing, and there was Primula stuffing her little face at the bait station. I made a beeline for her and she gave me a feint in one direction like a nimble halfback and then sprinted the other way, running quicksilver little circles around the patio furniture and the hunting blind. She's an agile little thing. Kyle was shouting, "Get her, Dad!" Eventually she tired of the game and I caught her in the back corner and carried her back to the fence and dropped her over onto our side. My side. As soon as her hooves hit the grass my little baby sped off to hide herself in the thicket. "Stay out of Jim and Klara's, you idiot!" I shouted after her.

"That was cool," said Kyle. "What's that tent for?"

"That's a hunting blind. Jim and Klara want to kill deer."

"Why?"

"Because they hate deer."

"So do I," said Kyle. "A deer bit me."

"She did not bite you," I said.

"She did!"

"Well now she's dead."

"Good!"

It's very difficult to describe how him saying that about Charlene made me feel. The emotions were many and violent and boiled up in a volcanic cauldron and I had just enough self-control to growl, "Get out of here! Get out of here before

I knock you down and stomp on your ugly little face, you little fucker!"

Sylvie said, "Trevor!" and pulled him against her, the back of his head between her breasts.

"I'm serious," I said.

"Let's go, Kyle," she said. "I'll talk to you later, Trevor, when you're rational."

She turned him by the shoulders and led him double-time through the carport toward the street. The volcano inside me spewed out, "Michael's got a secret!"

She stopped full stop. "What did you say?"

What impulse made me blurt that out? A pang of regret pierced my rage, but not enough to stop me. "Put Kyle in the car," I said.

"What? No way!" he protested.

"Yes. You will wait in the car," she said. She handed him her phone. "Play with this."

"The apps on your phone suck."

"Buy another app then."

"For real?"

She nodded. "You know my Apple ID. Buy anything that's not first-person shooter."

"Awww!" he whined. "All the ones I like are—"

"Get in the *fucking* car," she said, diamond-hard. His eyes went wide. He was well used to the word from me, but not from her.

"Come inside," I said to Sylvie.

We went to the desktop computer in the rec room downstairs. "I'm not going to say anything, I'm just going to show you," I said.

That old PC takes forever to fire up and function. We sat in matching beat-up swivel chairs we bought together at some office furniture auction years ago. Almost like old times. How many times had we sat in them doing mundane shit like taxes together?

"What's it about, Trevor?"

"Just wait."

"Just tell me."

"Just wait!!!"

Finally the spinney circular indicator of time's inevitable passage disappeared from the screen and three clicks later we saw six ugly seconds of infidelity. The quality was poor—the light from my phone reflecting back off the windowpane caused a double exposure effect, where you could make out my hands holding the phone in closeup, visible but ephemeral, like a ghostly veil, and beyond it, in less than ideal focus, Michael and Birgitta doing the nasty on the desk.

"What is it?" said Sylvie.

"Can't you tell?"

"No. It's all blurry."

I played it again, and cranked the volume. You could just hear Birgitta's voice.

"I'm still not sure what it is," said Sylvie.

"It's Michael and Birgitta fucking!"

"What? Trevor—"

"I'm telling you, Sylvie, that's his den, look at it!" I played it again. "His den, his desk, his ass, her legs! Look!" It was over that fast. I clicked on it again, and didn't say anything this time.

"Where did you get this?" she said.

"I shot it. Through the window."

"When?"

"I got super mad that you set up Randall to interrogate me the other night, so in my drunken state I thought it would be good to go to your place to give you a piece of my mind, but of course it was the middle of the night and when I got there the house was dark and sleeping except for one light in the den—"

"Show me again," she said.

This time I paused it just a split second before the end, just as Michael turned his head to look at the window. At the lens. Guilty! It was like those Crime Stoppers videos where the guy in the hoodie in the convenience store is identifiable by physique and body language more than facial features. If you knew Michael at all, you just knew this was Michael. To make the case even stronger I said, "I was there, Sylvie. I saw it with my own eyes. He's got varicose veins. You can almost see them here." I let my hand hover by the screen just below his flabby ass. Then it felt a bit too weird to be that close to his ass with my finger. Like I might catch something from it.

"It's very blurry," she said.

"I didn't mean to tell you like this," I said. "I didn't mean to blurt it out! I had a plan—I was going tell Michael I had

it, and make him promise to stop—make him promise to
treat you right."

"Fuck fuck fuck fuck fuck," she muttered, swivelling her
chair away from the computer and staring downward, like
her whole life teetered on some precipice, some razor's edge,
and she was about to slip. The free fall down the moun-
tainside would be long and painful and everything would
be smashed at the bottom but she wouldn't die. Instead she
would have to climb from the wreckage and clean herself
off and tend to her wounds and start all over from scratch.
Start now, basically.

Then suddenly there was Kyle coming through the door
waving Sylvie's phone, complaining, "I can't get your stupid
ID to work!" He stopped cold in front of that frozen image
on the computer screen, of Michael's grotesque face twisting
around above his naked backside, and Birgitta's legs in the
air. Both Sylvie and I shouted, "Get out of here!" and I slid
in my chair over to block the screen with my torso while
Sylvie leapt up and started shoving him out of the room, but
it was too late, there was no doubt he had seen the screen,
had absorbed it deeply and unfiltered in a heartbeat, and he
would never forget it.

I, for sure, will never forget the look on his face. Poor
little guy. All the rage and fury I'd felt for him a few minutes
earlier was erased in that instant, cancelled and replaced by
a deep and abiding wish he be allowed to grow and prosper
into a kind-hearted and decent human being. I'm so sorry
Kyle—you are eight years old and that is way too young to
chance upon the sordid revelation of that screen.

I fumbled for the mouse and clicked the image closed,
so the screen reverted to its regular wallpaper, which was a

blue-sky sunshine picture of me and Kyle and Melissa on a beach in San Diego after visiting Legoland, a photo taken by Sylvie in the sands of happier times. You cannot go back. Life keeps frogmarching you forward, like Sylvie had just frogmarched Kyle out the door. They were in the mudroom and I could hear him asking, "Why was Michael naked like that?" and Sylvie was saying, "That wasn't Michael, never you mind, let's just get your game set up here and then you go wait in the car." He didn't ask anything more, and it took a long aching chain of silent moments before she got her phone to where she could hand it to him and say, "There, it's downloading. Now go to the car."

In the voice of a grave little man trying to be brave he said, "Thanks mom." It was heartbreaking. I heard the door to the carport shut behind him and Sylvie came back into the rec room and burst into uncontrollable sobbing against my shoulder. I kept my arms at my sides because I felt like she didn't want arms around her. She wanted support but not encasement, if that makes sense.

Her crying lasted a long time.

Then she got control enough to step back and wipe at her wet face and say, "I'm such an idiot."

"No," I said.

"I don't know what to do."

"I shouldn't have told you. I was going to go to Michael with it, and tell him to smarten up."

"No," she said. "I'm glad you told." She took a deep breath, psyching herself to step out of the wreckage and back into the world with all its unsynchronized random demands and changeable plans going forward. "I've got to go," she said. "Kyle's got martial arts and we're already late." Then her lip got all trembly and she started to cry again, and through her tears she said, "Can you take him? I need to stay here for a while."

"Yeah sure. Best if you stay put." Her face looked red and wet and raw like a wound. I was feeling for my car keys when my phone dinged in my pocket. It was a text from Rolanda, reminding me we'd never set up our next appointment and saying she'd just had a sudden cancellation for 11 a.m. Like in an hour. She said something along the lines of she really felt the need to see me—a bit odd considering how our last meeting went. But what the hell. "What time does martial arts finish?" I said.

"Noon."

"Okay. I need to see my therapist at eleven. I can drop Kyle if you can pick him up?"

She nodded. "Good you've got a therapist," she said.

"Yeah. See you. You gonna be okay?" Dumb question.

She nodded. "I'm going to sit here for a bit and think about what to do. Then I'll get Kyle from martial arts, pick up Melissa from aquatics, and I'll have to take them home." The way she said "home" was like she didn't have one.

Kyle's face in the SUV looked small and vulnerable. I waved at him to get out and come get in my Honda. "Change of plan, bud."

He had Sylvie's phone in his hand. "What about this?"

"We'll leave it in her car. On her seat where she'll see it." No way was I going back inside to give it to her. Once you're out in the air, away from human suffering like that, so torn up and jagged, you keep a distance. Let her grieve in peace. Kyle was delaying, hypnotized by the little screen, trying to squeeze one last round out of his new game. I grabbed the phone from him to put it in her SUV myself when it dinged a text. You know how a new text shows up so you don't even have to open anything to see it? There it was, from Michael: "I'm feeling frisky. Where are you?" Nervy fucking slimeball! Double dipper! I wanted to crush the fucking phone, even as part of me was awestruck by the alpha-male ballsyness of this dude. I thought of texting back, "Go fuck Birgitta, if you haven't already today." That would have felt good. I didn't have the password.

Although it moves you through public space, a car is internally a very private space, a sealed box on wheels naturally suited for heart-to-heart conversations. How to broach it with the boy? I said, "Kyle, listen—I don't know what you saw or think you saw on the computer just now—"

"I didn't see anything," he said.

Okay. Maybe it's better if he blocks it out? His martial arts dojo is like five minutes away from the house, so anyhow if we were to slice open the wound there'd be no time to stitch it back up. No point getting into it, then. I felt relief, actually. Sleeping dogs and all that. When we got to the dojo I got out of the car. "You don't need to come in," he said.

I said, "I just want to give you hug."

He took a step back and without looking at me said, "Fuck off." Then he peeled past me to the entrance, and with the mighty pent-up power of ten grown men, he threw the big plate-glass door wide open.

"None of this is my fault!" I shouted after him. What a stupid thing to say. He didn't look back or anything, just disappeared inside.

I showed up at Rolanda's office with so much to talk about, starting with Primula almost dying from foxglove ingestion, and the cops getting on my case over it, and Crystal the deer killer messing up my mind by helping save Primula while still cold-bloodedly calculating how to kill Marlene and Darlene. Then there was the Michael video shattering Sylvie to bits, all because I couldn't keep my mouth shut, and Kyle who I'd wanted to trample to death—my own kid!—and next thing wanted to hug and nurture and protect, poor little bastard who didn't want a hug. But all of these things got forgotten as soon as I came into her waiting room because my mind was staggered by the fusillade of smells that hit my nostrils.

The waiting room was empty; I sat my ass down and listened through the wall to Rolanda and some other woman in the safe space having a serious heart to heart. Full blown emotional and psychological wounds were being ripped open, and it seemed to me that all humans, every single member of our species, suffers from some major or minor malady of the psyche. Is it the modern age, with all its stresses and distractions? Or did we always suffer like this, and the only difference is now we have labels? If you don't know the name for depression, do you know you're depressed? It's like paramedics—they've been pulling severed heads from car wrecks for what, a century now? And all of a sudden everyone knows what PTSD is and every second paramedic is on stress leave with PTSD. Or is modern life more gristly (grizzly?) because of high-speed collisions—peasant farmers tilling fields never saw blood and guts except in the slaughter of animals that they ate. They could prepare themselves psychologically for that, and justify it, and express gratitude to God and the animal for its sacrifice, but now we all live artificial lives, cut off from nature, and unconnected. Hunter-gatherers on the land, or peasant farmers tilling the soil by hand—do they get depressed? Do they wonder what's the point of it all? Or do they just carry on, knowing they are connected to something bigger, a part of some natural and sustaining system? I don't have answers, obviously, and partly I was thinking these thoughts just to distract myself from eavesdropping on the conversation coming through the wall, because the walls at Rolanda's are thin and my ears were twitching and focusing on the words that reached them quite beyond my ability to tell them not to. My sense of hearing is heightened these days too, and although I didn't want to, I could hear every word. Some stranger's private problems are not my business. To stop it I stuck my fingers in my ears and hummed, and that is how Rolanda and this woman found me as they emerged from the inner sanctum.

A bit of social awkwardness later—goodbye Betty, welcome Trevor—Rolanda shut the door behind her, and before she could say a word, I said, "You are pregnant!"

She kind of flushed and blushed and looked absolutely radiant and I felt a tremendous pang of remorse, like I wish I'd been the one to give her the seed a man gives a woman, so that little spark of life inside her would be half mine and I'd get to feel proud and virile and essential to someone else's existence, at least genetically. But my thoughts weren't all selfish—I also felt thrilled for her. She was surrounded by a spout of hormonal odours that just about knocked me on my ass. "I inhaled it as soon as I came in the waiting room," I told her. "But it was mixed up with that other woman's smell and I couldn't interpret who was responsible for what. But as soon as she left—Bingo! Rolanda's having a baby!"

"Well..." said Rolanda, a little shyly. "Part of the reason I was keen to reschedule our meeting..." Her voice trailed off, then the shyness burst like a dam and her face broke into a big smile. "I actually think you might be right," she said. "I'm pretty in touch with my body, and this is new and different. It's too early for a test to tell for sure, but some women say they just know it, as soon as they conceive, and I must be one of them! I can just feel it—like something major is going on. Something new." Her voice was like the singsong of a goddess, her usual professional demeanor of empathy for hire replaced by something more bubbly, more buoyant.

"Did you try it the way I told you?" I asked. "Like, in bed?"

Her eyes sparkled and she smiled a mischievous smile. "Yes!"

"Looking over your shoulder while he crouched behind making baby faces, and baby sounds?"

"Yes!"

"It must have worked!"

"Yes! I mean, at first when I told David about it, we were laughing—I mean it sounds so odd and eccentric that we had a giggle—but then later in the bedroom he acted it out, more just out of playfulness, more kidding around than serious, to make me laugh, and lighten the mood, but then I think it actually had some genuine effect—it melted something in me, and I was more receptive. He looked so cute!"

"Wow. That is awesome."

"You are on to something, Trevor."

"I know! It's great! I feel fantastic! Validation! Vindication! Can I ask you something?"

"Sure."

"Before he entered, did he lick your vulva?"

Her face fell a bit, and she got kind of self-conscious, like she suddenly remembered she had professional duties and standards to live up to and all that, and I'd gone too far. I said quickly, "Sorry—you don't have to answer that. But we were on such a roll!"

"No, it's okay," she said.

"It's what the stag does while he's back there making baby faces—he licks—I didn't tell you that last time because, well, it was weird enough as it was, right?"

"Definitely."

She was smiling again. We smiled at each other. Radiant reflections. I truly did feel validated and vindicated! My heightened senses could no longer be discounted as some strange self-generated delusion in my own head, but had proven themselves in the world beyond my imagination. They were real. They existed.

"I'd been wondering exactly how to diagnose you, or categorize you, and now, here I am thanking you," Rolanda said.

"Well I'm glad you've come around. I may need you," I said. I told her about pulling the foxglove out of that cranky geezer's flowerbed, and how the cops had visited, and now they had their eye on me, and how I wasn't even done—the real battle had not yet begun.

"What do you mean?"

"Crystal. The bow hunter. The night's coming soon when she'll try to kill Darlene and Marlene. There is no way that will be allowed to happen. I will not let anyone harm my tribe. If it's kill or be killed, so be it."

"Trevor, don't say that."

"I fucking mean it."

"Don't say that."

"Don't tell me what to say! Your job is to hear me out!"

"I can't let you advocate for violence, even in the face of violence. There must be a way out of this. A peaceful resolution that everyone can live with."

"I don't see it. Crystal needs her filthy lucre; she wants a return on her investment. She did compromise; she told me she'll spare Primula, although I don't trust her flunky—some guy named Sky, who I've never even met. She said she'll tell him to leave Primula alone, but still—guy makes a living slaying animals, what's a fawn to him? Nothing but an easier kill."

"The whole situation is very, messy," said Rolanda.

"No kidding. Oh yeah, you know what else is messy? Last time I saw Sylvie, she was sitting in my basement bawling her eyes out." I told her that whole story, starting with me being dragged from sleep by "Spare Me Your Platitudes!"—a nasty start to the day that got worse when Kyle said "Good!"

that Charlene was dead, and how I wanted to trample him underfoot, my own offspring, for saying that, but later when he burst in the rec room and saw the image from that secret video, of Michael frozen mid-thrust, all those feelings I'd had about hurting him got utterly inverted into tender concern that the poor kid is now scarred for life. "Do you think he's scarred for life?"

Rolanda said, "We can't know that. What we do know is kids nowadays are seeing porn and such online, earlier and earlier, and seven, eight or nine is not even uncommon anymore, apparently. The consequences of that will only be known in time. The particular image, the way you described, doesn't sound too horribly graphic. It was from the backside—"

"But it was Michael! He recognized Michael!"

"But not the *au pair*, though? He wouldn't have the context to put that part together."

"I don't know. Maybe. He only saw her legs."

"So he might naturally assume that's Sylvie. Do you think he even understands about sex yet?"

"I don't even know. I'm so disconnected."

"I wouldn't worry too much about him."

"But why would he deny having seen anything, and tell me to fuck off, and go running off?"

"Well you told me that just before that, when he said he was happy a deer died, you said some very unkind, almost cruel things to him. Maybe it was payback for that."

"Maybe."

"I'm more concerned for Sylvie. What is she going to do?"

"I can't take care of everyone," I said. "I've got Darlene, Marlene, and Primula to look after."

"But Sylvie's the mother of your children. In the coming days she's going to be sorting out what to do. Do you see a role for yourself in that process?"

"Jesus Christ, Rolanda, take my side!" I shouted it a bit loudly.

"Trevor, please. I am on your side."

"You sound like you're on her side! Let's take care of poor Sylvie. What's happening to her now is exactly what she put me through!"

"I'm trying to help you here. Long term, we need to set some goals for this therapy. I hope, when things settle, we can get to that. But things are not settled. Short term, things are very much up in the air. It would be good to be mentally prepared for things that might happen next," Rolanda said. "Sylvie may not want to stay with Michael anymore. She may ask to stay at your place, or have the kids stay at your place."

"The kids don't want to stay at my place."

"The kids may not get all their wishes."

"What about my wishes?"

"You were telling me just now about how you experienced such a wave of empathy, or sympathy, for Kyle today. Now is the time to focus on those emotions, which are helpful and healthy ones, and extend them to Melissa, and if you can find it in your heart, even to Sylvie."

"Oh that is such—" I was going to say bullshit, but stopped myself. My head was throbbing like you cannot believe, and I was rubbing frantically at the sore spots above my temples, two little swirling eddies of pain. "I'm tired," I said. "My head really, really hurts right now."

I heard someone enter the waiting room outside, and knew that our time was almost up. Supersmell of his scent wafting under the door told me he was a guy in his mid-thirties who smoked a lot of pot. Rolanda kind of shivered a little, as if she were shedding my story, with all its attendant emotions, and getting ready to sit through the next. I really don't know how therapists do it. One trainwreck after another, all day. I got up off the floor.

"I'm glad you're in my corner, Rolanda."

"Are you going home now?"

"Yeah."

"Will Sylvie be there?"

"No. She's got to collect the kids and ferry them around some more."

"Modern parenting."

"Yeah."

"And what are you doing with the rest of the day?"

"I'm going to look after my fawn. And write tons in the journal, like you asked me to. I like it now. Looking after deer and writing things down. Those two things are keeping me sane."

"I'm glad you're writing lots."

"Oh I am. I'm making sure to get it all down, in detail, laying out the whole story. Just in case things go off the rails."

PART IV

When I got back from Rolanda's I slung a hammock between two trees out back—that slinky kind of hammock that weighs nothing and looks like fishnet. Primula was not around, which put me on edge as I lay there, swaying a little in a breeze that set the leaves atremble overhead. I was thinking about how Sylvie and I bought the hammock in the Yucatan years ago, on our only vacation without the kids. We had a private balcony where we could hang it. Fond memories of us climbing into it in the moonlight filled my head. Her on top, obviously—poky nipples dangling to my lips, hammock swaying like a tease, making you work for it, not letting you get the leverage for the full-on piston-like thrusts a man so dearly craves. You want to bang away but you can't, so you compromise, and it becomes all about tiny movements in unison—better for her than me. She loved it. She was in control. Thinking about that stirred me up. I lay curled on my back like a shrimp, feeling my cock bloat and engorge like a bull elephant lifting its trunk to the heavens. Only thing missing was the mighty jungle trumpeting shriek of dominance and pleasure elephants make in Tarzan movies—Brap bra-brap BRAAAA-AAAAA-AAAAAPPP!!!!

Time passed, the sun skittered through the trees to cross the sky, and the day grew warmer while I daydreamed of Mexican beaches and bikini tan lines and petted the drumlin in my pants, kind of warily, like you'd pet a stranger's sleeping pit bull. Then I heard voices next door. Crystal was talking to Klara. I couldn't catch the words but Crystal was the alpha and Klara submissive and the words were just bullshit human banter. Crystal's fragrance came to me on the breeze and I thought, she is getting close to perfect, peak fertility, and my cock twitched and tried to flail about like a shark on the floor of a fishing boat but my jeans were a straitjacket. Then her scent filled my nostrils, my sinuses, my whole fucking brain, and I knew she was near me before I even heard or saw her.

I opened my eyes and there she was, looking down at me. You can't roll over in a hammock. I still had that urge, the civilized instinct to hide from her the lump in my pants.What could I do? I placed my hands over it, fingers interlocked lowdown like a horizontal choirboy. "How's the girl?" she said. She was wearing short blue gym shorts with white trim, and a tank top. So fine it was painful to look upon.

"I've given up chasing her around," I said. "She'll come to me when she's hungry."

She sniffed the air, lifting her head like a doe.

"It smells like deer over here," she said. "There's something about it. It's taking me back somewhere, to when I was a kid."

"Doe or stag?" I said. I don't know why.

"Good question. They're different, for sure. During the rut that musky smell of the stag gets overwhelming—I can remember being out in the woods with my dad and almost swooning." She sniffed the air again. "It's that smell. I do smell a stag."

"It's me," I said, and tried to slip out of that slinky fishnet hammock, but my feet got all twisted up in it like birds in netting. I put my palms on the ground and tried to kick myself free, which only made it worse, until all I could do was slump down on my back onto the grass, legs up and entangled, kicking feebly like a baby against bedsheets.

"Let me help you," she said, and she very calmly, very adroitly stepped up and pulled open the hammock like a whale's mouth, top lip up and bottom lip down, and my feet tumbled out to the ground. I lay in the grass looking up at her, wishing she would lay down beside me. That would have been so nice. Standing over me, hands on hips, she was the very essence of pure, unadulterated female swagger.

She said, "It looks like tonight is the night."

For a second I thought she was talking about sex, like, us having sex. I sat up expectantly. Then she said, "The camera's given me a good read on prime time for feeding next door. It's about one o'clock in the morning. They've lost enough of their natural suspicions about the blind—they're comfortable with it."

"Why did you have to bring that up?" I said. Why did she have to completely ruin the mood by reminding me she's a coldblooded deer killer? I could feel my blood-stuffed bone begin to ebb and dwindle, which surprised me, because lately it's been such a bad, bad boy with an iron-willed mind of its own, like that day Rolanda was ovulating in her office and I just about lost my mind on account of spiral emanations from the center of the universe, or to put it more bluntly, Stag Cock practically split the seams of my jeans in its overwhelming need to pump seed to make a baby. To prevent that from happening I had to jump up like an idiot and run out the door without even a goodbye. Well this time it wasn't like that, exactly. This time Stag Cock was telling me, not in words, but through the very blood we share, blood that was flowing into it and back out of it, circulating through my mind and body, *This is only a temporary retreat. She's getting oh so close—she'll be ovulating next time we meet.*

"I thought you'd like to know the plan, so you'd stay out of harm's way," said Crystal.

"Stay out? My whole plan is to get in harm's way. Harm is not going to happen!"

"I've told Sky about Primula—he'll be here tonight. I've got my bachelorette party to go to, remember? Well look here!"

My sweet and stupidly naive little fawn had appeared, and came running right up to her like a puppy looking for petting. Crystal started cooing at her and rubbing her neck and chest. It was a mutual girl-on-girl love-in, which disturbed me. "Don't touch her—don't let her get used to you!" I said.

"All right then," Crystal said. "I should go." But she hesitated. Something made her linger.

"If you weren't a killer I'd want you—to stay," I said.

She kind of arched an eyebrow but didn't say anything. Was she flattered? Bemused yet wary, I would call it. But that's only a guess and I could have been projecting. Primula continued to push and rub against her, the way a cat will polish human legs with the length of her smooth body. Maybe the little one sensed in Crystal something female or maternal I can't offer. A mother's scent, so redolent of home sweet home.

"You really like me, don't you sweetie?" Crystal said playfully. "Unfortunately, that's not good. Your daddy wants you all to himself."

"It's not like that," I said. "I don't want her consorting with someone whose intentions she doesn't understand."

"I've already told you she's safe with me."

"But the others aren't."

I got up off the ground and made a move to shoo Primula. All impulse, I grabbed her little black tail and tugged on it like a dog leash to pull her back and away from beautiful dangerous Crystal. Her two hind legs lifted right off the ground and she emitted an intense high-pitched squeal of pain and distress. I barked out an equally short note, not high-pitched but low, deep, like a grunt—not a sound I've ever made before. Crystal retreated a couple of steps.

"Don't be rough with her," she said. Primula ran off to a safe distance, then came circling back closer, tentatively.

"It didn't hurt," I said. "Just surprised her."

"You yanked her tail."

"For her own good!" I said. At that exact moment, guess who came through the carport into the back yard, her face a flood of tears?

Sylvie. She stopped abruptly, seeing I wasn't alone.

Jesus Christ. I thought it but didn't say it. Probably showed it in my face. I have enough on my plate.

"I'll be going now," Crystal said. She looked from Sylvie back to me. "See you later."

As she left she gave weepy-eyed Sylvie a wide birth, like any stranger would. You don't generally invite yourself to wipe the tears of someone you've never even been introduced to. You avert your eyes and tiptoe past. I think she might have muttered a gentle "Hey" on her way by, but if she did, Sylvie didn't acknowledge it. Crystal disappeared around the corner, leaving me with Sylvie's ragged wet face staring at me from fifteen feet.

"I put the hammock up," I said. Like she would care.

We saw Klara come out her back door and notice us, and study us, maybe picking up signs of distress in Sylvie's body language. She waved, and Sylvie waved, then turned her back to her and said, "Let's go inside."

"Good idea. Best get away from prying eyes."

didn't invite her upstairs. We stood in the mudroom and she gave me the lowdown. She'd picked up the kids from martial arts and aquatics and taken them home. Michael wasn't there, but Birgitta was in the kitchen getting lunch ready. First chance she got her alone, Sylvie said something neutral yet probing like, "Have you noticed anything weird lately, like bursts of light or camera flashes, coming in through the windows at night?"

Their eyes locked and Birgitta froze like a "deer in the headlights"—yes, Sylvie actually used that phrase to describe it. The Danish damsel knew the gig was up—she broke down and confessed to everything. Apparently for the past six weeks she and Michael have been doing the nasty on a regular basis, sometimes late at night in the house, sometimes on weekday afternoons on his boat at the yacht club. "It's so sickening!" Sylvie raged. "It's not like sneaking her off to some discreet, private rendezvous—those docks are public places, people parade along them like the runways of a fashion show. I can just see him leading Little Miss Denmark past his buddies on *their* boats, disappearing with her below deck while everyone has a giggle about it, everyone tells everyone else about it, and no one tells me!"

"I know what you're feeling," I said. "I've been there."

That stopped her cold for a sec. She said, "I'm really sorry, Trevor."

"Did you and him ever do it like that, on the boat, when you were still married to me?"

"Don't be cruel," she said.

I could have said, What goes around comes around. But why escalate?

"So what's the next step?"

"Well she has to leave, obviously. I told her she has to leave."

"What did she say?"

"She didn't put up a fight. She's just a ditzy kid and it was all a big lark. The intrigue of it—the sneaking around, having secrets. Now she's been busted, dragged into the light, she can see how sordid it all was."

"And what's Michael's excuse? He's old enough to know better."

"That's the thing—he's in meetings all day, to do with financing that big development on the water in Esquimalt."

"What, you can't bring yourself to disturb him over such a petty, minor detail as fucking the *au pair* right under your nose?"

"Don't raise your voice at me. Not now."

"I'm not." I dialed it back a bit just in case. "Anyway, Birgitta's probably texting him with the gory details."

"Shit. I hadn't thought of that," she said.

"You're better off telling him sooner than later."

"I'm going to text him."

"Saying what?"

"I need to see him as soon as possible." She gave me a pitiable look. "I need to ask you a favour."

"I knew it! Rolanda predicted this!"

"You haven't even heard what it—"

"If it gets messed up with Michael, you need a place to stay, right? I'm like, Plan B, right?"

"The kids have bedrooms here, and I can sleep down here, in the rec room, on the fold-out couch. I won't be in the way, I promise."

I shrugged like, *Que sera sera.* "If you must."

"Can I ask one thing? Upstairs? Is it clean?"

"What, you want me to tidy up for you?"

"No, but—"

"You know it's a fucking hovel up there," I said. "Don't push it."

She texted Michael and got one back immediately, saying he really needed to see her and could they meet ASAP, so she left for the showdown, leaving me alone, and it was suddenly very quiet, the quiet before the storm, the afternoon of the evening of the night the hunter is meant to strike. I was pissed at Sylvie for imposing the wreckage of her own life onto mine at such a crucial moment in time, worried she'd show up like a refugee from a war zone, in full retreat from Michael with two kids in tow at the worst possible moment, like if, for example, I was engaged in hand to hand combat with Sky. I'll tell you one thing—I wasn't about to clean the house for her. Let it rot and decay in its state of natural entropy. Let her scrub the fungus from the sink if it so offends her. But nightfall came, and the clock ticked on past ten, past eleven, and she never showed.

ky showed. Yes, Sky came in the darkness of night. It was about 11:30.

He tripped the motion-sensor above Jim and Klara's back door and his shadow spilled long and black over the bait station. He's a tall guy, dressed like any other normal twenty-something in jeans and a hoodie. He brought two crossbows with him, plus a quiver of arrows and a thermos of coffee. One thing I can tell you—I hated his smell. I smelled him fifty feet away, a mixture of coffee, tobacco, alcohol, and stale male sweat like gym socks, and because I hated his smell, I hated him too.

Jim came out to greet him and have a chat. I crept into the darkness of my carport to better observe and eavesdrop. I could hear Sky telling him deer were creatures of habit and the camera Crystal set up had confirmed their routine. "They feed here around one in the morning—three of them," he said. "Two smallish females and a fawn."

"That sounds right," said Jim. "You think you can get all three in one go?" He sounded downright gleeful at the thought of it.

"Not likely. Hit one and the other two will high-tail it, probably. It'll be more than one night's work, unless I'm lucky—stags will pretty much always take off like a shot, but sometimes does will just freeze up when they see one fall.

They stand stock still, not sure which way to run. That's why I've got two crossbows—they'll both be cocked, unlocked, ready to go."

"They're nice looking. High tech. How powerful are these things?" Jim asked.

"Oh they're plenty powerful," Sky said. "This one here is just about the fastest compound bow money can buy. It's got an arrow speed of 400 feet per second, if you can believe that. Here I'm shooting from, what? Ten, fifteen feet? We're talking a *micro-second*! Just like *Phooomp*!"

"I'm gonna stay up and watch from the window," Jim said.

"Keep the lights off. Keep it dark," said Sky. It worried me that he didn't say anything about sparing Primula. Maybe Crystal forgot to tell him, or maybe he just didn't want to bring it up with Jim. Maybe Crystal told him spare the fawn, but keep Jim in the dark about it?

"What about the motion detector?" said Jim. "It'll come on when they come—won't it spook them?"

"Most people have motion detectors around their house and the deer get totally used to them," said Sky. "In actual fact I think deer start to see it as a sign there's something good to eat—delectable leafy treats planted by humans."

"Huh. I put it up to scare them off."

"Has it been working?"

"No."

"Exactly," said Sky.

Crouched in the darkness, I still had no concrete plan in my head beyond keeping an eye out for the girls, and shooing them from Jim and Klara's if I should see them going there.

My big worry was there are four sides to their property, and realistically I could only keep a proper lookout on two sides at a time. I started to dwell on the worst-case scenario. What if I missed them coming in, and ran out too late? Wouldn't it be better to disrupt the hunt well in advance of that, like for example tie a rope to the hunting blind and pull the thing over? The problem with that is, Jim would for sure call the cops, and they might charge me this time, and take me in. Then who would look after my girls?

I decided this would be my strategy: If Marlene and Darlene came toward the bait station I would rush out of the darkness and grab the stilt-like metal posts of the blind and give it a Herculean shake!!! The thing would swing and sway like treetop branches in a high wind, and inside his tent Sky would stumble around off-kilter like a cruise ship passenger in hurricane seas, making it pretty much guaranteed he'd miss his shot. That'll work!

One in the morning was their expected chowtime, so there was still about an hour to go. Sixty minutes passes mighty slow in a quiet semi-illuminated suburb, where the world is outwardly calm, peaceful and at rest, but you, you're a ball of gut-knotted tension, getting ever more convinced that something awful is going to happen, and if it does, it's because you fucked up and didn't stop it. Sky had climbed up into his camouflaged tent; the flimsy fabric hiding him from view did nothing to prevent his smell from wafting over and violating my nostrils. I breathed through my mouth. From time to time I could hear him cough and fart. Otherwise all was still.

More time ticked past. Crouched in the carport I saw a raccoon go to the bait box and give it a sniff. It triggered Jim's motion detector, trundled under the hunting blind, and took a deep whiff of Sky. It almost seemed like it wanted to shimmy up the metal poles, but it experimented and decided they were too smooth and shiny. It wandered off and a minute later the light went out and it was dark again. Suburban dark, which isn't that dark, except for the deep black in the shadows of walls. I was getting cold and stiff, impatient and a little drowsy.

Then it happened. Darlene came down my driveway, Primula following behind. Darlene seemed to hesitate a bit, wondering what the hell I was doing in the carport in the middle of the night, but Primula was her usual blithe and carefree self, and came tippy-toeing right on up. She nuzzled against me, probably hoping for a bottle. To her I'm a bottle of milk. She made feed-me sounds, little pleading bleats in the silence of the night that sounded like a child crying. I shushed her, and I could hear Sky stirring in the blind.

Darlene circled the carport and walked unhurriedly towards the gate to Jim and Klara's yard, which they had left open. "Get away from there," I whispered, but Darlene kept going. In my carport there's some gardening stuff, some plant pots emptied of soil but still with some rocks in the bottom for drainage. I grabbed a couple of rocks and tossed them at Darlene. It worked—she altered her course, heading instead across Jim and Klara's front lawn. I was feeling good about that for just a second when suddenly the sensor light in the back yard kicked in and it lit up Marlene like an actress on a theatre stage, a few steps short of the bait station. She looked determined to get herself some of that delicious free snack.

"Jesus Christ, Marlene!" I shouted, and sprang into action, but unfortunately my carport has a two-foot high retaining wall on the side, and as I tried to vault it with stiff cold legs my foot caught the top of it and I tripped. I got up off the ground fast as I could and streaked through the open gate, which made Marlene jump back a few steps, but not far enough back to safety. I kept on, charging top speed, silent and swift, right up to the scaffolding poles, which I shook like Mighty Samson, metal scraping metal making a hideous screeching racket like a choir of dead children in Hell, and Marlene bolted over the back fence, gone.

From inside the blind Sky cursed a blue streak, and Jim came out of his house telling me to get the fuck off his property. For a few glorious seconds, I felt God-like and strong, the saviour of my flock, and raised my clenched fists above my head triumphantly. Then I noticed Primula was running little circles around the yard and there was a *phwap!!* sound from the blind and she fell to the ground like she'd been punched in the head.

he got to her feet, staggered but alive. An arrow had pierced her below the neck, just where shoulder meets foreshank, or that's what it looked like—the arrow tipped up and down, forward and back like a teeter-totter as she stumbled around the yard. She was crying like it was painful, but she wasn't dead. I was thinking, *She isn't dead! I can rescue her! All I gotta do is catch her, get the arrow out, stop the bleeding, everything will be fine!* Except she ran out the gate into my back yard, into the thicket and gone. "Primula! Come back!" I shouted. In the meantime, Sky opened the back flap of the blind and jumped down the ladder to the ground, clutching a crossbow and his quiver of arrows.

"Who the fuck are *you*?" he said. Jim came out his back door, and Sky said to him, "Who the fuck is this guy?"

"Crazy neighbour," said Jim. "Didn't Crystal tell you?"

"Oh yeah. Right. I thought she was kidding. Where'd the deer go? I think I got one. Did I get her?"

"You got her," said Jim. "She ran off."

"Shit!" said Sky. "Rule number one is finish the kill. I gotta go after her."

"She went thataway!" said Jim, pointing into the darkness of my thicket.

"I gotta go get my headlamp from my truck," said Sky.

"You shot her!" I shouted at him. "Crystal told you not to shoot the fawn!"

"Shit," he said, like he remembered now. "I got caught up in the moment."

"I'm going to kill *you*!" I howled, and I lowered my head and ran straight at him, but Sky is a nimble fucker and young—he sidestepped me like a matador and before I could turn or slow my momentum he tripped me, and down I went, hitting my head on Jim's outdoor patio table, which was glass-topped and metal edged.

The glass cracked but didn't shatter and my head hurt like hell. Tears clouded my eyes. The worst of it was, before I could get up Jim sat on top of me and yelled for Klara in the house to call the cops.

"Keep him here," said Sky. "I'm getting that headlamp and going tracking!" He made it sound like some awesome adventure, like instead of being sorry he was even glad it had happened like this. That enraged me so much that I twisted under Jim and raised myself up and bucked him off like a rodeo bronco, and the taste of my own tears reached my mouth and drove me mad. Jim yelled for Sky, and Sky turned back from his mission to the truck and the two of them circled me like a movable corral, keeping me penned while Jim yelled again for Klara to call the cops.

That camouflage-covered hunting blind loomed above us in the night, and I couldn't stand it, I had to bring it to the earth. I darted between my keepers and grabbed the scaffolding and rocked it back and forth, each push and pull adding to my power and lessening its resistance until finally with one last mighty heave I sent it toppling and crashing onto

Jim's patio table and chairs. It made such a fantastic unholy night-shattering racket that for the second time, I raised my arms above my head like a conqueror, the Genghis Khan of Gordon Head.

"What the hell is going on?"

A woman's voice. Crystal.

Yes it was Crystal, clattering in high heels around the side of the house from the street, stepping from dark shadow into the bright security light in a blindingly sky-blue dress, a Saturday-night party dress, with thin straps across her tanned shoulders and her hair tied up to show her graceful neck, so beautiful it hurt. As she hit the lawn her heels sank into it and she kicked off her shoes, standing barefoot and a bit tipsy. I could smell gin and tonic. I could also smell that she was fertile. It made me excited, and to drive certain thoughts from my mind I shook my head and body, back and forth like a dog shedding water.

"Primula! Primula! Primula!" I said to myself, to keep her in my mind. I didn't even know I was saying it out loud.

"What about her?" Crystal said.

"He shot her!"

"What? Sky?"

"By accident. I forgot," he said.

"Where is she?"

"She ran off. She's not dead."

"Well we have to find her and finish the job. Kills are required to be clean—no suffering!"

"You're not going to kill her," I said. "We can save her!"

"Where was she hit?"

"In the throat," Sky said. "I'm going to go get my head-lamp. I'll get her."

"No you're not," said Crystal. "Give me those." She took his crossbow and arrows. "You've done enough for one night. Get the headlamp and give it to me."

Ultraviolet and radiant in her party dress, she looked me up and down. When she slung the quiver of arrows over her shoulder the strap divided and defined her breasts. "If she can be saved, we'll save her. If not, then we'll have to put her down," she said.

In a moment of clarity, I said, "Wait for me, I'm going to get medical supplies." I ran over to my place and grabbed a flashlight, and what? Band-Aids? Antiseptic ointment? I remembered Sylvie always kept a first aid kit in the car and I got frantic looking for my keys and finally found them, and went to the carport and threw coats and kiddie toys and tire irons and booster cables out of the trunk until finally there it was, a little red bag the size of a shaving kit. When I slammed the trunk lid down, Crystal was standing at the end of the carport waiting for me. She had the headlamp on—she looked like a lighthouse, a statue of liberty, only dressed modern, in tight clothes, with that blinding bright light obscuring her face. "Come on!" she growled, "Time is crucial!"

I followed her toward the thicket. She moved with the grace of an athlete, like a huntress. "You've been drinking gin and tonics—several," I said. "Did you drive here? You shouldn't have been driving."

"I took a cab. I'm not that irresponsible. I was on my way home, when suddenly, I can't say why, I had the weirdest premonition, like something wasn't right over here. I told the cabbie to make a detour and swing by. We pulled up just in time to hear the blind come crashing down. Shit!"

"What?"

"I forgot to pay the cab."

"Well we're not going back!"

"No. Sky will get it. Let's focus. Does she have any favourite hiding spots back here, where she likes to settle?"

"She does, but in the dark, I can't say where. Even in daylight you can step on her before you see her."

"Maybe you should call out to her. Softly. Go ahead of me."

She made room on the narrow path for me, and as I passed by her I was nearly overcome by her proximity and her fragrance. It triggered memories of Charlene and her tarsals, and that led me to momentary grief and longing for one who died so young, but the present is where we live, and I was with a beautiful human who had perfumed herself for a night on the town, then perspired in high spirits on the dance floor with her celebratory girlfriends. The chemical mix was a chronicle of the evening, with the first part, the base, already so heady and intoxicating, supplemented by a new layer growing more potent, newly serious, announcing that a huntress was at the hunt—and enveloping its totality was a mighty, all-embracing aroma that screamed *I am fertile, I am ready, I am made to conceive.*

It was impossible to resist. I was ahead of her on the path but I turned back, and I bent my head toward her vulva, nostrils flaring.

"What are you doing?" she said. She reached a hand out to steer my head away from her, and found a stub above my temple big enough to wrap two fingers around like a joystick. She yanked it up and I straightened up. She let go and I touched the stubs in the hair above my temples. I had two of them, one on each side. Hard as rocks, yet pulsing, growing.

"They're growing," I said.

"Concentrate!" she said. "Find Primula!"

Of course! Primula. I took the lead along the path, and made a conscious effort to smell *forward*, not back. If anyone in the world could recognize Primula's unique smell it would be me! And sure enough, I did pick up her scent, and I knew we were on the right path, and it got stronger the deeper we went into the thicket, then kept on going through a gap in the ramshackle broken-down fence where my land meets the forest of the park.

"Primula! We're coming girl. Primula! Come to papa!"

I turned onto a little side path from the main path, like a rivulet from a river, off into the salal. I could actually smell her blood where she'd brushed the waxy evergreen leaves. "Come back here you little fucker," I called out.

My flashlight painted little slashes of clarity that made the rest of the darkness even darker. The light was fading from battery-rich clear blue to a softer yellow-orange haze illuminating the salal until it shone upon an apparition—what was it? Was it that half-doe, half-woman? The Woman of the Woods? Just for a second, I thought I saw doe-like eyes and long alabaster fingers cradling Primula. A scent filled my head and made my mouth emit a curious yelping sound, like a chained dog makes when it sees a loved one coming. "Hey!" I shouted like a human, and in one sudden motion she released the little fawn, guiding her towards me with the most gentle yet urgent of shoves, and she darted into the blackness, disappearing like a magician. I had to fight the urge to track her, an urge so strong I was nearly willing to leave Primula behind. But I didn't, I kept that sweet baby fawn in the weakening glow of my flashlight, and whispered gently, "Come here, you," and she came to me unsteadily, and then she saw Crystal with her brighter, more intrusive beam coming up behind me, and tried to dart for cover behind the trunk of a massive Douglas fir. But I had hold of her. She looked exhausted, ready to surrender. The arrow in her shoulder protruded with its fletching straight toward me, and I could see the other end, the head end, where it emerged through the skin underneath her. "Are you alright darling?" I murmured, and she gave a little bleat, as if to say, *This is really bad and I didn't do anything to deserve it.*

Crystal caught up with us, dimming her headlamp. It was still brighter than mine and Primula turned away from it. "Let me check her," Crystal said. She felt around the wound where the arrow came out. "I don't think it hit anything but loose skin."

"Turn your lamp right off," I said, and she did. Primula relaxed a little. "You poor thing," I said. "How are we going to get this thing out of you?" I ducked down and could see the arrowhead was about an inch across, impossible to pull back through the shoulder without ripping a bigger hole. "We need to break the shaft," I said. "What's it made out of?"

"Carbon fibre outer with an aluminum core," Crystal said.

"Fuck! We'd need a hacksaw."

"Yeah."

"Could I break the tip off?" I reached under her and up the shaft for the tip, and it sliced my finger like a razor. "Ouch!! Sharp motherfucker!"

"We'll have to carry her back to the house," said Crystal.

"Okay. Come here baby."

I scooped my little fawn into my loving arms and stood up straight. Crystal walked ahead of us with her headlamp on, and held my flashlight on her bum, pointed down behind her to illuminate the path for me. The light reflected off her calves, alternating with each step. Lovely, lovely calves leading me like a leash. I heard an odd noise behind us, like a song, or a lullaby, hummed by a closed mouth, musical but not exactly human. It was a beautiful song, very soothing, and I felt Primula go limp in my arms. The song comforted her, and it comforted me too, making me feel like whatever happened, we were doing our best, doing what was right. No need for worry or regret, no would've-should've-could'ves— just carry on, Trevor, it'll be okay. I turned around for a second to peer into the dark woods, hoping to catch at least a glimpse of the songstress, that wee fountainhead of peace and certainty, but that was a mistake, for the music stopped, and Primula started squirming, and Crystal, ahead of us, turned her head-beam around and flooded us with light that blinded, muttering tersely, "Keep coming!"

t wasn't that far, maybe a hundred metres back down the slope of Mount Doug to the property line, then another fifty through my thicket to the clearing at the back of the house. A smell reached me even before I saw them—the same two cops from the other night were talking to Sky and Jim and Klara in the back yard next door. Jim saw us first and said, "There they are."

I shouted, "We're busy here—life and death situation!" I turned to Crystal and said, "You think you can hold her while I get the saw?" She nodded. Primula was weak and trembling and put up no fight as I passed her into Crystal's arms.

"There's blood," she said worriedly.

"Mostly from me," I said, and held up my sliced finger. I wrapped it in my shirt tail and squeezed it to stop the bleeding, and ran in the house, to the workshop in the basement where I keep my tools. *Hacksaw, hacksaw, hacksaw, hacksaw—there you are!* By the time I got back outside, the five of them from next door had all come over, encircling Crystal, who sat on a lawn chair cradling Primula in her arms. The two cops I could see at a glance were mesmerized by the fine-looking woman with her hair all tousled and colour in her cheeks, bare-footed and encased in a dazzling party dress that was riding up her thighs, and they could openly gawk at her without her noticing because she was preoccupied with saving a cute little baby animal. Their vibe was like, *Let's take a breather and enjoy the show.* Hacksaw in hand, I had to break the circle and the mood by shouting, "Everybody back off!" and they did, but only a step or two, enough to let me through. I knelt down before her and found the arrow shaft under Primula's belly, and told Crystal to spread her legs wide to avoid the blade. Her dress slid up even higher on her thighs and when I grabbed the arrow Primula kicked—her hooves scraped Crystal's inner thigh and Crystal sucked in her breath but didn't loosen her grip, or cry out or complain, just muttered softly to that frightened little fawn, "It's okay baby, it's okay."

I sawed at the arrow, my bloody hand gripping the handle, so much adrenalin in me the job was quick, the arrow severed, and I reached under Primula and pulled out the shaft. She gave a little cry and I yelled at her, "Done!" and showed her the arrowhead on the broken shaft, and tossed it away, where it hit Jim in the leg and he recoiled and yelled, "Jesus Christ, man, I could get rabies or something!"

"Shut up!" I shouted, and said to Crystal, "Where's the first aid kit?"

She glanced around and said, "We left it in the woods."

"NO! Jesus Fucking Christ!"

"It's all right," she said. "All we need are some clean cloths and a tensile bandage. Do you have a tensile bandage? Like to wrap around a knee?"

"I do, I do!" I screamed. "Excuse me officers!" They stepped aside—they were quite obliging considering how I'd so recently toppled the hunting blind and pulverized Jim's patio furniture into a pile of wreckage. One of them said, "We'll need to talk to you, soon, though, bud." I liked the way he called me "bud" rather than the more formal "sir," although I think it was due to Crystal—he was playing to her, projecting himself as the casual, charming dude in uniform. I headed back into the house to grab a couple of facecloths from the hall closet and then to the bedroom hoping there were tensile bandages in the table on Sylvie's side of the bed—Sylvie's former side of the bed—because Sylvie used to keep them there after she got a sore knee playing squash. Sure enough they were there, untouched in the sixteen months since she'd vacated the premises—not just one, but a bounty of three, *Enough to wrap up Primula like an Egyptian Mummy if need be!* Back outside, the circle of five had closed in again on poor Primula and I yelled at everyone again to "Back off!" which they did, barely. Crystal and I switched places—I took over the holding and she did the wrapping, and before long the front end of that little fawn did look half-deer, half-Mummy. I was sitting in the chair cooing soft soothing words to her when Crystal gave me the look I imagine the doe gives the stag when he's making baby faces by her back door. We fell helplessly into each others' eyes just for a minute before one of the cops—the drinker—said, for the first time with an edge, "We need to talk to you, Trevor."

Crystal said, "How about I hold her while you guys go next door and sort things out?"

"Wait. I'll make her a bottle first, just in case."

So that's what happened. I went in and taped up my finger to stop the bleeding, prepared a bottle of goat milk and yogurt and warmed it 27 seconds in the microwave, and brought it out to Crystal, who by that time was alone. "I had to really growl at them that they were stressing her, to get them to go wait next door," she said.

"Thank you."

We looked at each other and it was like we shared something special. We cared about Primula, both of us. She took the bottle and brought it to Primula's lips, but the baby fawn showed no interest. "It's here if you want it," she said. Then she looked at me and smiled, like maybe she was saying it to me. *It's here if you want it.* Then she said, "You should go next door."

Amid the wreckage of the toppled blind and broken patio furniture, Jim was telling the cops I was a crazy son of a bitch, while Klara nodded and said "Uh huh," and Sky said the scaffolding barely missed him when it crashed and he was lucky to be alive. When they saw me coming, they toned it down, very Canadian of them, like they didn't want to insult me directly to my face, but it was still three against one while the two cops listened and took notes.

I denied nothing. How could I? The evidence was scattered all around. I tried to remain outwardly dignified and contrite, although I could feel my nostrils flaring and pulsing eruptions at my temples. The worst thing would be if the cops took me in, so to avoid that, I promised to fix everything. "I don't know what a hunting blind costs, but I'm good for it," I said. "Plus whatever Sky earns for a night's work, plus I'll replace the patio furniture, which was rusty and rickety to begin with, but now you'll get something shiny and new."

"The lawn is all chewed up," Jim said.

"I think you need to consider counselling," said Klara. "If no charges are to be laid, I think counselling is something you should promise to commit to."

"Who says no charges are to be laid?" said Jim. "I want charges laid."

"I'm good with counselling, I'm already getting some with Rolanda," I said. "I swear I'll get lots of fresh counselling from her. I swear on a stack of Bibles to pay all costs and damages, stay out of your yard, do more and deeper counselling to get a grip, work on my interpersonal social skills, and just generally calm down and behave myself."

"And leave deer alone," said one of the cops. The boozer. I wish I knew their names.

"What do you mean?"

"I mean, if people have a legal permit that gives them the right to cull a deer, don't decide you have a right to get involved. You don't."

"Okay. For sure. I promise," I lied.

Just then the radio on his chest started to squawk about a house party in Broadmead with drunken teenage disturbance of the peace threatening to spiral into anarchy on leafy suburban streets, and they told me they needed to attend to that but they weren't going anywhere until I promised one more time to stay cool for the rest of the night. I promised. "We'll swing by later and hopefully everyone's gone to bed," they said. Jim was not happy with that, but what could he do?

"Stay off my land," he said, as the cops walked away.

"Scout's honour," I said.

ky followed me back to my place to talk to Crystal. Primula quivered and shook at the sight of him like she knew he was the perp. She struggled to break free from Crystal's arms but she held her, soothed her, and then told Sky to collect the weaponry and go home. He picked up the bow and the quiver and lingered, putting his own spin on what had happened, laying the blame on me for rattling him around like bingo balls in the blind. Crystal told him "Bugger off home," which made me giggle, and Sky shot me a dirty look as he left, as if I was getting off far too lightly. And suddenly I did feel light—light-headed, dreamy, happy—Marlene and Darlene were unharmed and in hiding, and my little adopted fawn had been saved, and was nestled before me in Crystal's lovely arms. A half-moon came out from behind clouds for the first time all evening and turned her blue dress a deep aquamarine, like a Polynesian shoreline. "All's well that ends well," I said happily. Crystal said, "This is more like a midsummer night's dream."

She looked so beautiful in that special light of night that it made my heart swell with some feeling like fulfilment, or accomplishment, as if Primula were our child, Crystal the mother, and me the proud papa.

"Do you think we should take her to a vet?" she said. Notice she said "we." That felt so right.

"There's no vet open now."

"Yeah there is—there's a 24-hour animal hospital over by Mayfair Mall, in behind where Future Shop used to be."

"The stress would kill her—all the bright lights and sounds in there, and the overwhelming smell of dogs." Just thinking of multiple dog smells made me shiver in disgust.

"But some antibiotics would do her good."

"We'll make a little bed for her, and watch over her here. The wound's pretty clean, I hope. Two small holes—not like gaping slashes that need stitched up."

"I suppose you're right."

"You want me to take her?" I said.

"No. She's settled right now. Are her eyes open?"

"No."

"Then let her sleep," she said.

"What should I do?"

She gestured to the hammock. "Climb in there. You can spell me in a bit, then I'll be on my way."

So I lay down, watching the two of them seem to rise and fall as the hammock swayed and settled. I closed my eyes and soon I dreamt a dream, a tense dream of being hunted in the dark forest and snared in a trap that strung me up by a leg, the way cattle hang in a slaughterhouse. A hunter pushed me by the shoulder to spin me around, and I opened my eyes to see Crystal touching me to wake me, making the hammock swing ever so slightly.

"You were kicking and calling out," she said.

"Where's Primula?"

"I set her down in the long grass over there. My ass was killing me in that plastic lawn chair."

"I'm sorry about your ass."

"It's okay."

"Did I sleep for long?"

"Maybe an hour." She seemed a bit disoriented, looking down at me. "There's something about your smell," she said. "It's triggering something."

"Good, or bad?"

"Good—I know! I know exactly what it is now!" She was smiling wide and her teeth shone white in the moonlight. "It's like it's exactly that time—I'm twelve, the first time my dad took me on a hunt, driving his pickup on old logging trails in the woods above Cowichan Lake, and we stopped and got out, and walked to his favourite crossing, and then we sat, and sat, and sat some more, in silence, for just the longest time ever, which was absolute agony, the waiting, and then suddenly it happened so fast—he brought the gun up and shot—so out of nowhere—just BAM! I saw the stag buckling, its legs giving out, it fell down and it felt so wrong to hurt it, to harm it, I felt something so wrong was happening, but it was too late to go backwards in time. Normally when you've shot a deer, you don't chase it, because they'll run away, sometimes for miles with a broken leg or a mortal wound. So you wait, and watch, and give the animal a respectful distance as it dies. This stag was so close, it jumped out of the woods practically on top of us, and got shot at such close range, and went down so fast, tried to get up and couldn't, that we could see it all, close up. Dad said we still had to wait till we were sure it was dead, and then we came and stood over him. It was my first time being close to a stag like that, a huge beautiful being, every bit as complex as you or me, and he wasn't dead after all, there he was, breathing in weak little gulps. It was heartbreaking, really, watching the life force fade out of him, watching his eyes go from panic, to calm, to nothing, and I cried, broken-hearted, like I'd lost someone I loved…"

She put out a hand to gently touch my head above the temple. "What are these?" She felt one of the nodes pushing through my skin and above my hair there. "They're growing—it's grown like at least another inch on each side. They're velvety, like antlers."

"They're handlebars," I said. "Climb aboard."

That made her smile.

"No seriously, climb in with me."

She did. She straddled me on the hammock.

I'm having a hard time holding this pen to the page right now. Just remembering. Holy fuck! It was so intense! I'm shaking and shimmying and tingling even now. She hiked her dress and lowered herself onto me and inhaled me at my neck, and she growled, like an animal growls, like I've never heard from a woman, and I responded with the strangest yelping sounds that turned into deep bass notes like a ship's horn on a fog-shrouded night, and I can't say for sure it was her or me, but her panties got pushed aside and my jeans got popped and the zipper parted like an earthquake splitting a highway. Stag Cock sprang free and proud, screaming *I will now seize my destiny!!!* and he entered her, I entered her, *we* entered her and I only wish the right and proper words existed to convey to you the kaleidoscopical nature of the thermonuclear explosion—it was not just me exploding, not just Stag Cock, not just my body, mind, soul, but the whole fucking universe, so powerful and strange and beyond my ken, and I made more of those yelping sounds, the strangest yelping sounds ever—were they really coming from my mouth?—like a donkey braying, only undomesticated, tortured, orgasmic. Crystal didn't flinch or pull away but instead took it all deeply and pressed herself hard against me, she pushed her hips and vulva against me like she wanted to absorb me, subsume me, give as good as she got, and it all joined and melted and bubbled and boiled together down there, smoking hot and soaking wet, I could smell her wetness and mine mixing up together and the scent of it drove me out of this world! Yes. Yes. Yes! *Yes! Yes!! Here it comes. Here it comes!! Climax! Climmmaaaaax!!!!*

Then comes the void; you breathe hard to catch your breath, deep jagged gulping breaths that slowly lengthen and soften until you hear the sounds of the world again, the quiet hum of suburban night, and you come back into the day-to-day of human life, and you ask, *Did that really just happen?*

And you acknowledge something powerful happened.

And what do you do with it, and where do you go?

She was nuzzling against me, laying her head on my chest, a hand reaching up to hold one of the nubs by my temple, smoothing and petting the velvet of it. "I'm going to nap now," she said. Laying back, breathing calmly and feeling ever so much at peace, I looked into the thicket and saw someone watching me—that doe woman, wood spirit, half doe, studying me: The Woman of the Woods. Had she seen the whole thing? She looked confused, unsettled, like she had a million questions. She saw I could see her, acknowledged it with the slightest tilt of her neck and head. Then she raised a hand and let it fall softly across her face, and closed her eyes, a gesture I took to mean *Go to sleep now Trevor, Go to sleep.*

PART V

Then it was morning, long after dawn. The hammock swinging crazily woke me up as Crystal climbed out. She pulled and tugged at her dress trying to straighten it, but it was all creases and wrinkles. There was a stain all along the hem at the front. Her face had a big red circle on one cheek, an indented, crosshatched pattern from being squished against the hair on my chest.

"Is your house locked?" she said. She did not look at me lovingly. She did not look at me at all.

"No."

She went inside, and came out a few minutes later looking marginally less dishevelled.

"Would you like anything? Coffee?" I said.

"No."

"Are you all right?"

"Yes." Probably the sunlight made the creases of her dress more pronounced than the bathroom mirror had, and she tried to rub them out, turning her back to me so I wouldn't see her hands as they pressed downward over the curves of her breasts and thighs. There was a bigger stain on the backside, but I didn't tell her that.

"I was quite drunk last night," she said.

"You seemed pretty together to me. You did a great job tracking Primula, and patching her up."

"Yeah. I guess I did. Before that I had a lot to drink, and I'm feeling it now." She scratched one foot with the other. "Have you seen my shoes?"

"No." I stretched in the hammock, toes straight like a cliff-diver, trying to maintain the contentment bestowed upon me by a good deep sleep which was fading a little because her flustered vibe was carving slices off my peace of mind. "I think you kicked them off next door."

"And my purse? I had a little purse?"

"Next door again, maybe? That's where all hell broke loose. Definitely a strange night."

"What time is it?" Now there was definite agitation in her voice.

"I have no clue."

"I need to be somewhere at nine."

"It's Sunday morning—it can't be that urgent."

"It is. I've got to pick up my kid."

"I didn't even know you had a kid."

"I do—a girl. She's twelve. She's at her dad's house."

"Hey—mine's eleven, almost twelve." I was feeling—what was I feeling? Childlike, just then. Newborn. Carefree, like that mighty blast in the night had ejaculated all the cares and worries from my body and left a blank slate of innocence, like a baby's.

"I'm going to look for my purse," she said.

I watched her go into Jim and Klara's back yard, kind of sneaky-like, like she didn't want them to see her. She poked at the rubble of the hunting blind. I got up and stretched some more and looked around for Primula. No sign of her anywhere. I started to worry. Shit. Earthly cares already kicking in again. I felt bad that Crystal and I had got it on and passed out and forgot about the right thing to do, which would have been taking alternating turns of monitoring our injured baby.

Crystal came back with her shoes but no purse.

"Probably Klara found it and took it inside," I said.

"Fuck," she said. "I can't knock on her door like this."

"Want me to?"

She looked at me as if I was nuts.

"I've got to get home."

"Here's a plan," I said. "I'll lend you my car. You can bring it back later."

"Would you? That would be great."

"Sure. No problem."

"No strings attached, though, right?"

"What do you mean?"

"Well," she said. "There's still more work to be done next door. I don't get paid until the job is done."

The hairs stood up all over my body.

"I can't believe I'm hearing this," I said.

"Can we talk about it later?" she said. "Please can I have the keys? I'm in deep shit if I'm late."

"You're going like that?"

"I'll zip home and change." She thought for a sec. "Fuck! My house keys are in the purse. Can you lend me a screwdriver? I'll pop the screen off a window and get in that way."

"You're pretty resourceful."

"I'm a farmgirl, remember?"

went and found my keys and a screwdriver, and she took them and drove off. I went back in the thicket and started calling out for Primula, nostrils dilated, fully wide—I was smelling more than looking. There were so many, many odours separating themselves out for recognition, for individual inspection in my sinuses. Something has changed in my brain, and I wonder if I will ever be the same. Then Primula's smell made itself known: baby deer, dried blood, the sweat of Crystal's palms and the tiniest historical hint of Sylvie on the tensile bandage. My nose led me to her. My little fawn huddled down among ferns in the leafy shade of an alder. Around and about her was that other scent, half human, half doe, intermingled, inseparable, perplexing, fascinating. *Who are you?* Smells intrigue me now—this one above all others. Like a riddle, demanding to be solved.

rimula let me pick her up and carry her back to the house, and sat quietly under the hammock while I got her breakfast. She wasn't lively but she didn't look sick either. She drank her goatmilk well. I'd just stuck a second bottle into her mouth when I heard a vehicle slide into the carport. Not Crystal returning the car—this was a bigger beast, and when the engine cut out, the tell-tale glide of a sliding side door told me it was a van.

Kyle came around the corner first, followed by Sylvie, and lastly a resentful-looking Melissa. Primula turned her head to check them out. Seeing her bandaged, Kyle yelled out, "What happened to her?" She shivered a little nervously, but stayed put.

"Shh. Softly," I said. "She had an accident. She got shot with an arrow."

"No way! Where is it?"

"We pulled it out. That's why she's wrapped up like this."

The three of them gathered around me like gawkers before the Pieta. "Shouldn't you take her to a vet or something?" said Sylvie.

"Are you worried about her, or do you just want her out of here?" I said.

"I'm worried," she said. "Honestly. I don't always have ulterior motives."

"We have to stay here now," said Kyle.

"Oh really?"

"Mommy's super-mad at Michael."

"Shut up Kyle!" Melissa shouted. Primula jumped and squirmed in my arms.

"Don't shout," I said. "You'll disturb her."

"I'll shout if I want!"

"Shhhh!"

"Everyone's always telling me what to do but no one ever asks me what I want!" She burst into tears and ran in the house, slamming the door so hard that Primula broke free and skittered toward the thicket.

"It's all right, baby-girl," I called to her. "Don't leave my sight, please."

To my surprise she didn't. Almost as if she understood me, she stopped and settled in the shade beneath the hammock.

"Kyle, go inside and watch an episode," Sylvie said.

"Two episodes," he said.

"Whatever! Stare at Netflix until your eyes drop out of your head."

"What if Melissa got there first?"

"Negotiate. Just go. I need to talk to your dad."

He went inside.

"He is getting more and more of a handful," she said.

"They pick up on negative energy."

We looked at each other. Friends, lovers, enemies, parents, complex flesh-and-blood excreters of odours. So many things we were. Why did I even think that? Did each role have a scent? That is how I sensed them. Sorted them.

Sylvie began to cry. In spite of everything I couldn't hate her. "What happened?" I asked.

"He came home from his meeting, and at first he was all contrite and supplicating—Birgitta had made herself scarce, but she must have texted him to warn him of the shit-storm waiting for him." She took a deep breath. "So he'd had time to prep, to prepare his defense. He's a great talker. So smooth—he just *loooves* the sound of his own voice, and his favourite subject is himself—painting himself as this wonderful man of honour, but also a man of intense, unbridled passions, who knew better, of course he did, but he was tempted. Tempted by her 'relentless teasing'—that was his exact term for it."

"Well, it's an apology, at least. That's good."

"Not so good. He's a scumbag."

"What else did he say?"

"He's a bastard."

"But what did he say?"

"He said maybe we could have an arrangement."

"Uh oh."

"Yeah. Like an open marriage." She wiped at her eyes with the back of her hand. "And I said, 'We don't even have a marriage yet, and now you want an *open* marriage?' Then he reminded me that up until a little while back, I wasn't legally divorced from you, so who was the one playing around in marriage?"

"Nasty."

"Then he got this squinty, calculating look in his eye and said, for us to be considered common-law husband and wife, we need to live together for two years, and it's only been sixteen months, so therefore under the law, if we were to split, he owes me nothing financially. What the fuck is *that*?"

"Nasty, that's what that is."

"He wouldn't even agree that Birgitta should leave. He was like, 'Let's try to sort things out, we're all adults here.'"

"Technically."

"I couldn't stay. What could I do?"

Primula chose that moment to get up from under the hammock and was headed to the side of the house. "Don't go out to the street," I yelled. I scooted over to cut her off near the carport. "You stay back here." Now I could see the van Sylvie had arrived in—a Volkswagen Westphalia I'd never seen before. "Where'd you get the wheels?" I said.

"It's Michael's. Part of his Tofino-surfer-dude fantasy. Most of the time it sits in his garage. It holds lots of luggage and stuff." I could see mounds of clothes piled in the back; her and the kids must have emptied closets and drawers and just chucked it all in.

"Does it have a stove and sink?"

"I think so. Probably."

"Do they work?"

"Trevor, I don't know," she said irritably. She wiped at her eyes, like if I said one more thing to add to the indignity of it all, the waterworks would gush again.

"All right," I said. "Why don't you go inside and make us a cup of tea? Bring one out to me—I wanna stay here and keep an eye on Primula."

"Thank you," she said.

"Don't worry about it."

"Your arms look hairier."

"I know. My legs too. And my body. Pretty much every-where."

"Ticks could hide on you," she said.

"Don't be paranoid."

"I'm careful, not paranoid," she said. "I made a stop on the way here, to pick up something, for Primula."

"Like what? Like a present?"

"Kind of. It's in the van. It's a tick collar. Slip it on and she's protected for up to three months. It's meant for dogs—they didn't have one for deer."

"Are you insane? She's a newborn fawn, with a vulnerable, underdeveloped immune system, and you want me to go tighten a band of toxic shit around her neck?"

"Yes. If she's going to be in and around the house, then yes, I do. There might already be ticks in the house. Are there ticks in the house, do you think?"

"Sylvie. Listen. Just accept that not everything is going your way right now. Ticks are the least of your worries, so don't worry about ticks."

"That's not very comforting," she said.

"I'm giving you my home. Take comfort in that."

She gave a faint smile. Never in my life have I seen her look so defeated, exhausted and small. "I'm sorry," she said. "I've given you another thing to nurse back to health."

I didn't take the bait. No promises on that. We heard a noise next door. Jim was coming out to survey the wreckage. She ducked her head like she didn't want to be seen.

"I'm going to check on the kids," she said.

"Good plan. And forget the tea. I'll have coffee."

Jim was taking photos with his cell phone. Nothing for it but to go over and make peace.

The sun glinted off splintered shards of patio table top. They looked like readymade weapons, like you could just pick one up off the lawn and drive it like a stake through a vampire's heart. Jim was squinting at his phone and didn't notice me until I was right at his shoulder. He jumped back, shuddering in fright. "You shouldn't sneak up on people like that!" I inhaled fear in his sweat, like lifting the lid off a pot of minced garlic.

"What did you tell the cops?" he said.

"What do you mean?"

"Last night, you listed a bunch of things you promised to do, and one of those things was to stay out of my yard!"

"I forgot I said that."

"Well you did! I'm not talking to you until you're on your side of the fence. Otherwise I'm on the phone RIGHT NOW telling those officers you're violating one of your conditions. It's called trespass, Trevor!"

I raised a hand to—to what? Not to hit him—after sweet ejaculatory catharsis last night, and the deep sweet sleep afterward, I felt done with violent urges against Jimbo. No, my hand just hovered around in the air up by my head until it found a handhold to settle it, grasping the velvety stub above my temple. Those stubs are growing fast! Can I call them what they are? Antlers. I've got antlers. Holding onto one calmed me even more. Velvet smooth outside, hard inside.

Bowing to Jim's wishes, I went out his gate and scooted around to my side of that ridiculous three-foot chain-link courtesy fence that delineates our legal territories and keeps anarchy from raining down upon us, which proved to Jim I'm still human, and he relaxed a little. Surveying the litter of his lawn, I told him, "The damage doesn't look as bad as I thought last night. Maybe the hunting blind can just be lifted upright, get some bolts retightened, and be good as new. Some of that fabric will need mending."

"I don't need your advice," he said.

"I'll pay all repairs. I want to reiterate that. All expenses for the lawn, patio furniture, and the blind, plus I'll pay you back whatever you've given Crystal so far, and pay her whatever you still owe her."

"I don't owe Crystal anything more until she gets a result," said Jim. "And I still expect a result."

That rattled my Buddhistic calm. Made my hair bristle. Made me snort. Klara came out their back door.

"Hello Trevor," she said. She came over close to me at the fence.

"Trevor, I've been thinking maybe we'll call the whole thing off."

"What!" said Jim.

"I don't have the stomach for open warfare," she said. "I don't think I slept all night. And seeing that little fawn all bandaged up—"

"We are not calling this off, we are seeing it through!" said Jim.

"We're going to talk about it," said Klara.

"My ass we are! There will be no compromise."

I heard a door open behind me and turned to see Sylvie stepping out into the carport, bringing my cup of coffee. She was watching it so as not to spill, then lifted her eyes and saw Klara with me, and retreated into the house.

"Was that Sylvie?" said Klara.

"You know it was."

"She went back inside."

"So it seems."

"She's come for a visit?"

"Leave her out of it," I said.

Suddenly she gushed, "Here's the little fawn!"

Primula had come out of the thicket and came gambolling over to the fence, still wrapped in that tensile bandage but looking pretty damn energetic. "Look at you," Klara cooed. "I can't believe you want to hang around humans, after all that's happened to you!"

"I'm her meal ticket," I said.

"There's a gentle side to you, Trevor," she said. "I'm trying to focus on that."

"How 'bout we focus on this side of the fence?" Jim said. "Focus on the wreckage."

"We need to talk, Jim."

"We are not—backing—down," he said. He was seething.

"If you'll excuse us," she said, "We'll go have a chat." To Primula she said, "Bye sweetie."

Jim just glared.

I told Primula to stay put, I'd be back in a minute, and then I went in the house. Kyle was glued to Netflix in the rec room and Sylvie was upstairs cleaning the kitchen. "I don't know how you live like this," she said.

"There's no one to complain, usually."

"Here's the tick collar I was talking about." She handed me a package with a picture on it of a perfectly groomed sheepdog looking happy as hell. A plastic window below it allowed you to see the product: a rubbery white coil resembling an albino snake.

"You don't give up, do you?" I said. I flipped it over and checked out the fine print. "It says to wear rubber gloves when you put it on your pet. If it touches your skin it says to wash immediately, did you know that? I bet if I google it, it'll tell me it causes ADHD in kids! Human kids!"

She snatched it back from me and threw it onto the counter like, *End of discussion, for now.*

"What is with your hair?" she said. "You've got weird prongs growing out of it."

"Those are my antlers." It felt so good to say that. To take ownership of them.

Her phone rang, a jangly little pop song sample. She pulled it from her back pocket, checked it, and said, "Michael." Then she scurried down the hall to the master bedroom for privacy. Thank God. I definitely did not want to have to listen to that. I looked out the living room window toward the street and saw Crystal pull up in my old Honda and get out. She'd changed into jeans and a tank top and her hair was wet from a shower. She gave me a little wave and then cut diagonally across my lawn toward Jim and Klara's place.

Through the bedroom door came sounds of Sylvie's righteous rage but I couldn't hear the words.

I thought, *Chill woman. There's a price for everything.*

Then I thought, *Humans. They are strange. I don't feel like one.*

Melissa came out of her bedroom, which is opposite the master bedroom and listened to her mother howling through the closed door. She saw I could see her, and it made her mad. I lack words or gestures to soothe eleven-year-old girl misery. I went outside because I needed to be outside. Driven from my own house? No. Who wants a house anyway? I want open spaces.

It's better outside. Primula was curled up near the hammock, so I got in the hammock on my back, knees up. I became aware for the first time that last night's fireworks with Crystal had left massive cum stains all over my pants. Mostly around the crotch. Dried now. Did it bother me? No. My cock was dormant. That explosion had left a void, like a bomb blast leaves a crater. The rut was over for another year. I'd done my duty. Impregnated a female. Had I? If I have, would that be good or bad? Crystal carrying my kid. Good, bad—either way it was fate, now, not choice. I will live with what the Gods ordain. I remembered how I knew Rolanda had conceived a child just by the smell of her, then remembered there was none of that telltale pregnant scent from Crystal this morning. What did that mean? Maybe conception takes time? Wait and see. In the meantime, nap. Sleepy time, Trevor.

It was a short nap I think but when I woke up, the sun had moved higher in the sky and Primula had disappeared somewhere, and Crystal had appeared with Jim and Klara in their back yard. I sat up to look at them and could tell from their body language that Jim had won the battle with Klara. He was still on the warpath. Klara was withdrawn, like a non-combatant. Crystal was carrying on with Jim like an accomplice. She'd found her purse and had it slung over her shoulder. It looked funny on her because it was a little glittery thing meant for going out to nightclubs. I got out of the hammock feeling groggy, like I wanted to go lie down in the thicket and sleep a really deep long satisfying sleep again. They saw me and I heard Crystal say, "I'll talk to him."

She came over.

"I need to give you back your car keys," she said. "Thanks again for that."

My nostrils stretched wide as sink stoppers and relayed the information that Crystal was not with child. She still radiated fertile readiness.

"Jim wants you to finish the job, does he?" I said.

"How did you know?" She tried to sound playful. Didn't work.

"I'm going to make you an offer," I said. "Since you've already agreed to spare Primula, I'll pay the full fee for you to spare Marlene and Darlene too. I'm going to refund Jim the money he's paid so far, and pay you whatever he still owes you. I'll double it—double what he still owes. End of story."

"I appreciate that," she said. "That's very kind. But there are other things to consider—consequences for leaving the job unfinished. I can't advertise—I've got to keep a low profile, otherwise the animal rights types and tree huggers are all over me. I can't just put myself up on Yelp and wait for the reviews to roll in. The business is discreet by nature—it's dependent on positive word of mouth. On satisfied customers."

"Oh yeah, real discreet—like a hit man. An exterminator."

"This is my first job in Saanich since the new bylaw came in. I need it to be a success. I need Jim to tell his friends about it."

"Jim doesn't have any friends."

"I have a lot of financial issues right now," she said. "I'm a single mom, with an ex who is no help whatsoever. In fact he has major issues. I had to leave my daughter at his place last night, which I promised myself I would never do, but I'm a bridesmaid so I couldn't miss the bachelorette party, and the sleepover I set up for her fell through. I told her I'd pick her up at nine sharp, and that's why I woke this morning and rushed off. I had a promise to keep."

"It did seem a bit weird. Like night and day," I said.

"Daylight brought me back to reality," she said.

"The night was soooo intense, though."

She blushed a little, like the thought of it embarrassed her. "It was too much of too much," she said. "On top of drinking and dancing and alcohol, and all the excitement of rescuing that adorable fawn, cradling that poor little needy thing on my lap, and her smell—and something else, in the air—it was too much."

"It was the most intense thing I ever felt in my life," I said. "I wish I had words to explain it to you—how the universe exploded—"

She cut me off. "I'm just glad I have an IUD in. Not that you thought to ask about anything like that."

"No. I was in the rut."

"Do you read the *Times-Colonist*?" she said.

"Not cover to cover."

"You might have seen something about my daughter in there, how I'm trying to crowd-source for her. She has stage-two lymphoma."

"Lymphoma. That's like cancer, right?"

"Uh huh."

"But stage two. That means it was caught early."

"Yes."

"So she's not going to die."

"Survival rates are like, better than 90 percent, so we're hopeful," she said. "But the treatments are in Vancouver at Sick Kids, so the ferry and hotel costs are like, sinking us. That's why I have to take jobs like this, and why I need to finish them."

"I'm really sorry to hear that. That's awful," I said. "But so is what you're doing here. Don't think of what you're doing here as a means to an end, no matter how noble and justifiable the end is. Think about Marlene and Darlene, living, breathing, happy, until you came along and killed them."

"Culled them," she said. "I don't take the killing part lightly, I told you that. I told you how I used to go hunting with my dad? Did I tell you that after a successful take-down, he would make me say thank you, to be grateful for the food it would give us. I always did. I said a prayer to the Deer Gods for taking one of their herd. I still do that."

"How nice. I'm sure they appreciate it. Don't you think the Deer Gods might be trying to tell you something right now? Don't you think the universe is all connected, and if you're doing one weird, cruel thing over here, you can't compartmentalize—it's going to spill over into the rest of your life, until you're treading water in a sea of weird cruelty?"

"I respect what you're saying," she said. "And I do promise to reflect on it, when I have time to catch my breath. But for now, I've got short-term goals, caused by short-term cash flows, and I've gotta get through this."

"Why can't we turn it into a win-win? I pay you off, I pay you double, you win, the deer win. Why do the deer always have to lose?"

"They don't always lose. They're wily, they're clever, they're elusive—that's their strength, their secret weapon. It's magical the way they vanish sometimes."

Vanish?

Vanish.

Something happened to me when she said that word, something triggered in my mind. Suddenly there was an out, an answer, a new idea. *Escape!* Of course! So obvious! Darlene, Marlene, Primula and me—we need to vanish! In a jolt of bright light it was all so clear—I'd been fighting humans, not just one or two, but the entire species, and that is a war I will never win. Deer live by flight, not fight! They evade trouble, not confront it. To live in peace they need to go unnoticed, undetected. Struggling to make a life for yourself on the margins of suburban fucking Saanich puts every deer born to it smackdab in the crosshairs of the most voracious prey species on the planet. Proximity to humans is the problem. The solution is so simple: When in danger, get the hell outta Dodge!

ylvie was in the kitchen. I told her I needed her help. Then I started yelling, "Kyle, Melissa, get up here! I need to talk to you!" They both yelled "What?" from distant rooms, as if I should go to them. Why is it family pushes your buttons like no one else pushes your buttons? I went down and shut off Netflix and dragged Kyle upstairs by his scrawny little bicep. My hand still fits around it nice and snug, I got a good grip. He didn't like getting yanked up the stairs and was whining profusely, which made Melissa come out of her room to identify the source of his pain. She had been painting her nails blue and the killer nail polish had a killer smell that was not just an insult to my sinuses, it was an endangerment. The toxins in it just about blew my head off. Did it get me high? Maybe. Fucked me up, but what could I do but carry on?

"Now we're all here, I have something important," I said.

"What's it about?" said Melissa.

"Sit down and I'll tell you. Sit. Are you ready?"

"Are you keeping those things stuck on your head permanently?"

"They are antlers. And yes. Or no. I'm thinking they'll go through their natural life cycle and drop off."

"How long does that take?"

"I think about ten months. The process repeats itself yearly. Just sit. Listen. Sit." They did, finally. Deep breath.

"I'm bequeathing this house to Sylvie, and you guys can live here without me."

"Trevor—"

"No listen, really. Listen. There's a *quid pro quo*. The van. I want the van."

"The van in the carport? Michael's van?" Sylvie asked.

"Yes. That is correct."

"Done."

Wow. That was too easy. I'd expected more give and take. More of a skirmish.

"I feel like we should shake on it," I said, half joking. Sylvie stood up. We shook hands, one-quarter joking.

"Good. Great. Now there's one more *quid pro quo*. In this part of it, you might get your hands dirty. All of you."

Sylvie made a face, Kyle looked slightly frightened, and Melissa surprised me by saying, "This could be interesting." Like, she needed an adventure in her life, not just watching other kids have one on YouTube. Good for her.

"Okay, here's the deal. I'm going to take that van, and I'm going to point it north toward Port Hardy, drive right up the Island, and when I'm way past Campbell River somewhere I'm going to go down some obscure logging road and find a remote, hospitable spot, open the side door, and let Marlene, Darlene, and Primula out."

"You're going to put deer in the van?" Sylvie asked.

"Yes."

"And drive them hundreds of kilometers?"

"Yes."

"How will you get them in the van?" asked Kyle.

"Ah Ha! That's what I need you for, my boy. And you, and you!"

They all three looked a bit stunned for a sec. Then Sylvie said, "I can't"; Kyle said, "I won't"; and Melissa said, "You mean we'd be like, beaters? Drive them toward the trap?"

"Exactly!"

"How do you know about that?" said Sylvie.

"I read lots of books set in olden times. I like the Medieval," said Melissa.

"Good. So you know how it works. We create a funnel to the van door, and working together, as a team of shepherds, we circle around behind them and guide them into the funnel."

"Don't make it sound easy," said Sylvie. "Don't even make it sound doable."

"It's doable."

"As long as we get behind them at the start," Melissa said.

"Atta girl."

The two of us worked on Sylvie until she came onboard, still grudging and reluctant. Kyle took a lot more coaxing, and the promise of new Lego. Now we were a team, sort of. "Here's the plan," I said. "Well, first of all, Darlene and Marlene need to come into the back yard. That's when we kick into gear and get to work. Until then, keep your shoes on even in the house, and be ready to go at a moment's notice. I don't want to have to round you up."

"We have to round *them* up," said Melissa.

"Nice one. We should go out and practice. I'll tell you guys where to stand, and what to do."

Practice we did. It went sort of okay. There were no actual deer yet, which removed the wildness element and made it too close to a stately procession, like a wedding rehearsal with an imaginary bride and groom—they'll walk this way, and we'll gather along behind. Sylvie and Melissa would need to discreetly get behind them and then drive them forward. Not drive them, exactly, I made that clear, or even herd them, but rather encourage them, guide them. Kyle would be at one corner of the house with a six-foot piece of irrigation pipe to wave around like a lance, so as to look like someone you'd give a wide berth to. The lance made him feel safer, but I worried it might be too scary for the girls, the deer girls I mean, the does, and would spook them. I rigged up a rope line from the trees to his corner of the house, about twenty feet worth, and then hung some tarps and blankets on it to make a temporary wall. It was eight feet high and came almost to the ground, so it worked good, like a serious barrier. That meant Kyle wasn't essential on that side anymore, so I shifted him over to work with me on the other side, over by the three-foot fence between our house and Jim and Klara's. The gap there was the last major escape route before the funnel. The funnel was a hockey net and a couple of big sheets of plywood I had on hand, leftovers from home handyman projects. You make do.

While we practiced, Crystal was poking around in the back yard next door. Then she went and sat in the shade of Jim and Klara's house like she was waiting for something, and she was—Sky showed up, and they stood the hunting blind back up—I was right, it wasn't really that damaged. They tightened it up and laid the planks of the floor back, and then Sky left. I thought she'd gone with him but it turned out she was in the tent sewing it up. I saw her get out while I was on the edge of the thicket showing Sylvie exactly where I wanted her to go. Melissa was a natural, but Sylvie was stiff—frozen up by tick dread. I went in the house and found that tick collar in the kitchen, brought it out to her and told her to put it on around her pant leg—it would fit snug above the knee. She of course refused—I knew she would. But my tactic worked—by declining the offer of protection, walking unprotected in the thicket became her own choice.

So. We got that sorted, and then here was Crystal by the fence asking what was going on. I told her my new plan, and guess what? She got all perky and said, "Great idea. If you take them away up-Island, that counts as removal for me. The contract doesn't actually say I have to kill them, I just have to remove them."

"Why didn't you say that before?" I said.

"I've never done it like that. No one ever asked. Relocating deer would be complicated and expensive. You'd need a place to legally re-release them, which I don't know of. Plus you'd probably need a permit, but you can't get one because the government doesn't have it set up that way."

"Fuck permits, we're doing it," I said.

"Do you want to help us?" said Melissa.

"Okay," said Crystal.

What could I say? The more the merrier. We practiced some more, five of us now, making changes in strategy based on advice from Crystal. Melissa glommed onto Crystal like she was a goddess huntress—she thought Crystal should be in charge because she knew how to stalk deer and how not to spook them, and I could feel my authority waning as Crystal became more assertive in her opinions. She had serious doubts about our chances of encircling wild animals and started talking up tranquillizer darts, which planted seeds of doubt in my mind. Plus, by then the sensory overload and weird high I'd gotten from Melissa's nail polish had worn off, so reality suddenly looked daunting as hell.

Daunting, yes, but did I give in to negativity? No, I did not. I moved a little way off from the others and shook my head so rapidly back and forth that my lips flapped like flags in a storm, shedding negativity with great force. I shouted out my troubles—I was really shouting! Not human words, wilder sounds meant to expel demons of doubt, like an exorcism. It felt really great, and as I came down from it, snorting away in satisfaction, Sylvie, keeping her distance, said, "You look deranged."

"I'm feeling good," I said. "I'm becoming who I'm meant to be."

rimula had been hanging around watching us, treating it all as a game. Getting her in the van would be no problem—Crystal or I could just pick her up. Marlene and Darlene would not be so easy, but somehow I had faith—I felt if they trusted me, and understood I had their best interests at heart, it would work out. All we could do was wait for them to show up.

Hours went by. Kyle went in to binge on Netflix and Melissa begged Crystal to let her try out her crossbow. Crystal went and got it and instructed her on how to use it. Safety first and all that. She fired an arrow into a piece of plywood, and the thunderclap when it struck the wood stung my eardrums. I told them to put it away—there was no way Marlene and Darlene were going to come anywhere near the place with a racket like that going on.

Sylvie had gone in to get dinner ready, and then Crystal started to get antsy like she couldn't hang out all day waiting for Marlene and Darlene to show, and she went in the house to use the bathroom and didn't come out for awhile, and I left Melissa to keep watch and went in to see what was up. The house smelled of meat, which I have no stomach for these days. In the kitchen, the two women were hugging teary-eyed—Crystal had been telling her about her daughter, near the same age as Melissa, but with stage-two cancer. I felt bad about what I'd said earlier, when Crystal had told me about that—I hadn't shown much sympathy, even suggesting it was the Deer Gods invoking the law of karma on her, which is another way of saying, *It's your own damn fault.* They dried their eyes and composed themselves at the sight of me, and then Sylvie said, "You should really change those pants." And, "Whew, you smell."

I decided to have a super-quick shower—I was running water down my evermore hairy torso and legs when there was a knock on the door and Melissa shouted, "The deer are here!"

In panic mode and dripping wet, I whipped on my boxers and caught a glimpse of myself in the mirror that made me think, *Who's that bigfoot in the bathing suit?* before I pulled on pants and a t-shirt and ran barefoot downstairs to the back door. The four of them were huddled by the window looking out at Marlene and Darlene on the edge of the thicket.

"Do you think they're going to settle in and sit down?" Crystal said.

"It's not their usual time for that," I said. "They might just be passing through. Usually they go through the carport, but that's blocked by the van and the funnel. If they notice that, they might back away right now. I think we need to get out there, get around behind them. Do it now!"

"Okay," said Crystal. "When we practiced, we started from being in position. How do we get in position?"

"There's Primula. She likes you. You go to her and play with her," I said. "That should distract the girls. Sylvie, Melissa, you go out the front door, then around the side past the wall of sheets, then into the thicket behind them. Then you start walking them forward, very gingerly, toward the carport. Kyle, you come with me. We'll cover the left flank by the fence."

Day was diminishing into soupy grey light. Crystal went out and called softly. Primula Poppins came bounding to her like Bambi in bandages. It was easy enough for Crystal to draw her off to the side by the sheets. Kyle and I slipped out and headed to our positions by the fence. Marlene and Darlene watched us, hyper-alert. Kyle hissed, "I forgot my piece of pipe!"

"Shhh! It's all right. Just be quiet."

We saw Melissa and Sylvie enter the thicket from the backside of the wall of sheets. Marlene and Darlene saw them too, and definitely did not like it. The girls started walking forward, urging the deer girls to move ahead of them, fully out of the thicket and into the long grass of the yard, with its trampled patches here and there. Marlene swivelled her ears madly and broke into a trot, which made Darlene do likewise. I could smell their fear, which made me make a noise I didn't know I had, a soothing noise made with my mouth closed, coming out of my throat and through my nose.

Did it settle them? It drew them towards me, I think, but then everything went to shit as they came close and Kyle got spooked. He screamed "Get away from me!" in his high-pitched panicked kid voice, and abandoned his post in favour of running to hide behind his father. Darlene perceived a suddenly undefended gap along the three-foot fence, and bounded over it in a split-second with her tail raised to display her airborne ass. Marlene did likewise, two steps behind her. They doubled back to the corner of Jim and Klara's yard, and jumped the fence into the thicket. They were gone. Crap.

Melissa started yelling at Kyle, calling him an idiot and other choice terms in the eleven-year-old idiom, but I told her to can it, it wasn't his fault. "Those deer weren't about to be led meekly into a plywood-sided funnel, especially one dead-ending at a Volkswagen Westphalia," I said. I could see now what a pipedream it had been. Getting them to surrender their freedom would have required manhandling them with physical force well beyond our levels of strength and bravery.

"Now what?" said Sylvie.

"I think it's time to talk about tranquillizer darts," said Crystal.

"Can I go in and watch Netflix now?" asked Kyle.

"Go," I said. What to do?

"Have you ever shot tranquillizer darts before?" Sylvie asked Crystal, and then Melissa suddenly cried out, "Look!"

She was pointing toward the thicket.

Darlene and Marlene came tiptoeing out of the trees toward us, in an oddly stately, fearless, and trusting manner. Their ears looked peculiar—not pricked up and swivelling on alert, but drooped down, like nothing mattered, like they didn't have a care in the world. Behind them, shepherding them, was her. That half-doe, that half-woman. The Woman of the Woods. For the first time she was showing herself to the world, fully, completely. She looked Christ-like—you know those paintings where Christ stands in radiant dayglo robes, with his palms lowered and open at his sides, like a godlike daycare worker herding children in from recess? That was her vibe. Saintly, Noble, Poised, Proud, Calm, all these things and more, wrapped in a glowing aura not to be questioned or denied. Marlene and Darlene were under her spell, and Primula too. She darted to her and pranced little circles around her, jumping up and licking her hands.

She was Christ-like, yes, but without the robes. Unclothed she was, but not naked—a thin pelt of fur covered her legs, her sex, her belly, and the hint of breasts on her chest, which were not relevant or irrelevant, they just *were*. She stood upright like a human, but walked on tiptoes, like a ballerina. Her face was without hair, her olive skin flushing pink, her brown eyes oversized like a doe's.

Melissa said, "Is she real?"

"She's real," I said.

"Get out of the way," said Crystal, steering Sylvie and Melissa away from the entrance of the carport and into the back yard. That left me alone to greet them. As Darlene walked past, I ran a hand along her backbone, and she let me, she didn't even flinch. Then Marlene sauntered by, stopping for a moment to sniff at my tarsals. Behind them, encircled by hop-skipping Primula, came the doe-woman. She passed right by me without a glance, leading them to the open door of the Westphalia. Soft persuasive sounds from her throat made them step up inside that confined, unfamiliar space, without the slightest hint of worry or delay. Primula hopped in next like it was a game to play.

Then the woman-doe looked at me for the first time with those big brown eyes, and said, "Do it shut."

"What?"

"Shut. Do It."

I shut the door. Through the side panel window the girls looked a bit anxious. Three was a crowd in there.

"You go inside," she said.

"In the house?"

"No. Inside this."

I nodded. I opened the door and got in the driver's seat. She walked around the front of the van to the passenger side door, put a hand on the handle, and looked confused by it. I stretched across and opened it from the inside. Stretched out fully I could just push it open a crack. "Now swing it open," I said.

With the door wide she put her foot in, testing the floor's solidity. Then she slid her bum onto the seat, and put her other foot in. "Is it right?" she said.

I nodded.

"Close it now?"

I nodded.

She pulled the door shut. Her fingers, long and willowy, looked like they would sway in a breeze. As if the bones within them were still soft and forming.

We looked at each other. She was close to me and I was close to her. Not just the physical proximity, I'm talking about the mind. We were close. I felt understood.

"Now we go away," she said.

"That is right," I said.

"Far away."

"You got it."

I turned the ignition and strapped the seatbelt across my shoulder. She watched as it clicked in place by my hip.

"I must do?"

"Yes. It's behind your shoulder there."

She reached back and pulled it forward across her body, looking amazed and pleased with herself. She got it pulled down near where it buckled but couldn't slot it in. I reached over to help her, and our hands touched. Electric. She recoiled, but then brought her hand back, and let me take her fingers and guide the buckle home. Her skin was soft as a baby's.

We drove away. I didn't look back at the homestead.

For a minute we drove in silence. We were just turning onto Cedar Hill Road when she said, "Feel not good." She was pulling at the seat belt. "Feel like trap."

"You'll get used to it. It's actually safer this way. I'm Trevor, by the way."

I know that sounds very casual, but I was tingling. Every inch of me was vibrating.

"I know," she said. "I watch you many times. Hear people say, 'Trevor.'"

"I've seen you a few times too."

"I let you, only few times."

"Do you have a name?"

"Name?

"Like 'Trevor.'"

"No. New words come each day. Wake up, new words in head. New things. Like never before. But no name. Deer have no name. We know each other."

"Do you want to choose a name?"

"Like people name?"

"Yes. A human word for you."

"Human? Human names choosed, or gived?"

"Usually gived. Given."

"Then you give."

"Me? That's a lot of responsibility. I don't know you well enough." By now we'd crossed most of Saanich and were at the end of McKenzie, about to hit the highway. "Okay. I'll try. Tell me something that you like. Something that pleases you. Your name should be something you like."

"I like food."

"Yes, but something more specific."

"I like sleep."

"Those are things everyone likes. I'm talking about something that appeals to you, personally. Like something you like to look at, maybe?"

"I like to look at hummingbird fly."

"Me too! Okay! We're going to call you 'Hummingbird.' That can be your human name."

"Not human, not yet. Get more close to human. I feel it. Like you—you get more close to deer."

"I know! That's right! We're like mirror images."

She looked puzzled.

"Do you know what a mirror is?" I twisted the rear-view mirror towards her so she could see herself. She let out a weird snort of shock through her nostrils. The girls in back shifted uneasily, like they might stand up. She murmured a soft sound, a lovely, soothing sound like a magic spell, and they calmed down. She studied her face in the mirror.

"That me?"

"That's you."

"Look strange," she said.

"No, you don't. Not strange—unfinished. Like everything is in flux. When you're done, I bet you'll look amazing."

"You too unfinished. In flux."

"Is that what you think is happening? I'm going one way, you the other?"

"That is why I watch you. Only you."

"I'm still more human than you, and you're more deer than me, right? Do you think we'll meet eventually, come together smackdab in the middle?"

"We not same."

"Not yet. But someday? We'll meet someday, in the middle, and be the same?"

"Things not happen, I don't know them. Only can know things that happen."

"Try. It's called guessing, or imagining. Do you think we'll meet?"

"I try now." She made a face like it hurt to think that hard. "What happen, coming. It's new for me. Feels funny. I see we meet, for a small time. Then we pass by."

"What? No!" I shouted. In the back the girls jumped up and skittered around. Hummingbird made that gentle magic-spell sound again and they calmed down. "I was thinking we'd meet up right exactly in the middle, and stick there like equals and everything would be fucking awesome." I turned to meet her eyes. That puzzled look again, like she didn't understand wishes or have fantasies yet. She could only see what was most likely. I said, "If I keep moving deer-ward past you, and you keep moving the other way past me, if I become fully a stag and you become fully human—Oh my God, is that what's going to happen?"

"I watch over you. Like you watch over those three. I watch over four."

"But we don't know for sure what will happen!" I said. "We might stick! We might stay half-deer half-human, like the pictures on Pinterest. We might stay perfectly aligned!"

"That is not now. Only now is now."

"I get you. I know where you're coming from. Deer never think about tomorrow, right?" She gave me the puzzled look again. I said, "You know, like the sun will go down tonight, and then it will come up again, and that's tomorrow. Can you imagine that?"

Her eyes narrowed, and then went wide, deep and glassy. "I can! I can do!" She gestured to the three in back. "They do not, but I can!"

"Good. Great. If you keep evolving, I'm going to teach you so much. How to talk, eat, dress yourself, drive, read and write—"

"I never see read and write."

"Don't worry about it. You're not ready yet. Getting closer every day. Someday, if it all goes as you say, I might have hooves for hands and I'll need to dictate to you. It'll be your slender fingers that scribble my thoughts in my journal. My last human thoughts, before I have a stag mind."

"We move very fast," she said. For a sec I thought she meant the things we were talking about were overwhelming her mind, then I realised we were on the Island Highway, blazing north past Costco at super speed. 100 klicks an hour. She looked exhilarated.

"Something you should know about humans—they like to plan. Plan A, Plan B, we cover every eventuality," I said. "Right now, the only plan is to drive for about ten hours until we're up by Port McNeil or Port Hardy somewhere, and turn off onto a logging road, and get well off the highway and find a lake with water fit to drink, and park the van. Then we'll let the girls out and help them settle in and live in a van by a lake. Then we'll make some plans, and wait and see whether we need plan A, B, C or D."

"I see it," she said excitedly. "I understand!"

"Good."

"What's it called?"

"What's what called?"

"Things not come yet. But coming."

"The future. It's called the future."

"It's so good," she said. "Such a good thing to think of."

Printed in Great Britain
by Amazon

10036983R00157